Dress Rehearsal

Lorna Hill wrote her first sto[...] [...]
after watching Pavlova dan[...] [...]castle. Her
daughter, Vicki, aged ten, discovered one of these stories
and was so delighted by it that Lorna Hill wrote several
more and they were published. Vicki trained as a ballet
dancer at Sadler's Wells and from her letters Mrs Hill
was able to gain the knowledge which forms the background of the 'Wells' stories.

Sadler's Wells Series

Lorna Hill

Dress
Rehearsal

Piper Books

To Mrs Morgan, with love

First published 1959 by Evans Brothers Ltd as *Dress-Rehearsal*
This revised Piper edition published 1992 by Pan Macmillan Children's Books,
Cavaye Place, London SW10 9PG

9 8 7 6 5 4 3 2 1

ISBN 0 330 32137 4

Edited by Treld Pelkey Bicknell

Phototypeset by Intype, London

Printed and bound in England by Clays Ltd, St Ives plc

Contents

Part One

Chapter 1

Nona

Nona Browning stood on her own two feet at the age of five years. Doctors and nurses crowded round her. For the last six months they had waited patiently for this moment and had almost given up hope – except for the fact that doctors never give up hope – and now the miracle had happened . . .

But I must go back to the very beginning – to one New Year's Eve in a Northern industrial town, when a woman was brought into the Casualty Ward of Kenton Road Hospital suffering from shock and exposure. She had been found lying unconscious in the snow under the arches of one of the many bridges over the River Tyne, and it was obvious that she was very ill indeed. At midnight, just when the church bells were ringing in the New Year, her baby was born – a girl. Next day, the nurse whose duty it was to take down the names and addresses and other details concerning the patients tried to question her. The father of the baby – where was he? What was his name? His employment?

'He was a bad lot,' said the woman weakly. 'Left me flat. Never sent me a penny-piece – not that I would have taken anything from him. Never want to see him again . . . ' Her voice tailed away to a whisper, and she moved her head from side to side on the pillow, her dark hair accentuating the extreme pallor of her face.

'Well, dear, that's up to you,' said the white-capped nurse, 'but you must tell me who is your nearest of kin. Your father or mother, maybe,' she added helpfully.

'I haven't got any nearest of kin,' answered the woman, without opening her eyes. 'My father and mother died long ago.'

'But you must have *someone*, dear,' insisted the young nurse. 'Everyone has *someone*. Try to think.'

'I'm too tired to think, and it isn't any use,' moaned the woman. 'I've told you – I haven't anyone belonging to me.'

'Well, who do you want us to communicate with if – when –' she had been going to say 'if anything happens to you,' but hastily changed it to 'when you're well enough to go home.'

The woman turned her face to the wall.

'I haven't any home,' she said.

'You must have lived *somewhere*, dear,' persisted the nurse.

But the woman had fallen asleep, her thin cheek, now flushed with fever, resting on her hand.

The young nurse shrugged her shoulders, and went off to find someone more responsible.

'Can't get a thing out of the casualty in Number 7,' she said to the Ward Sister. 'She insists she hasn't any nearest of kin.'

'Maybe she hasn't, poor thing,' answered the Ward Sister, who had seen enough of life in the big hospital to learn not to be surprised at anything. 'Don't worry her just now, Nurse Macarthy. We can try later on.'

But the opportunity never came. After taking one look at her baby, the woman turned her face to the wall once

8

more, and closed her eyes. By the time the nurse had run for the Ward Sister, and the latter had hurried for the doctor, the casualty in Number 7 was dead.

'Just as though one look at her baby had killed her,' said the young nurse afterwards in the Staff Room. 'And no wonder! *I* shouldn't like to be the mother of a creature like that! It's my opinion,' she went on, 'that it's a changeling.'

'A changeling?' echoed Sister Browning. 'What on earth's that? An old superstition, I suppose?'

'Well, and what if it is? They do say in Ireland that a child born with a hare-lip is a changeling, left by the wee folk in exchange for the mother's own bonny babe. Now if this poor creature isn't the unfortunate child of some leprechaun, my name isn't Molly Macarthy! Talk about ugly!'

Sister Browning, creeping noiselessly into the Children's Ward later that night before she went to bed, looked down into the crib where the dead woman's baby lay, and felt strangely moved. The child was lying wide awake, and its eyes were fixed upon her – dark, mysterious eyes, quite unlike the misty blue ones of most newly born infants. It didn't cry either, and its fingers closed tightly round hers when she put her hand under the blanket to see if it was warm. It was as though it clung to her for life.

'Poor baby!' she said with a sigh of pity. 'I'm afraid you won't find the world a very hospitable place – and all for no fault of your own.'

The next day the hospital was electrified by the news that Sister Browning had told Matron she intended to adopt the orphaned baby with the hare-lip.

'Well, I hope you know what you are doing, Sister Browning,' said Nurse Mallory, who had just come on duty and was feeling at odds with all the world, as well she might at half-past five in the morning. 'It's not only the hare-lip that's wrong with it, you know. It'll be a cripple as well.'

'I know that,' answered Sister Browning gently. 'All the more need, surely, for the poor child to have a good home and someone to look after it, and as I'm due to retire at the end of the month it'll be something for me to do.'

'You're incorrigible, Sister,' said Nurse Heversham, bustling down the corridor with an armful of hot-water bottles. 'Just when you're due for a let-up – and you're none too strong yourself, you know, after your operation – just when you might take things easy, you go and saddle yourself with *this*!'

'I know very well what I'm doing,' repeated Sister Browning, firmly.

One and all they disapproved of her action, and didn't hesitate to tell her so. Only the Matron – a far-sighted and sensitive woman – understood (even if she didn't altogether approve, mainly because of the state of Sister Browning's health). She knew that nursing was Sister Browning's whole life, and that without it she would pine away. As it was – well, it would give the baby a few years of gentle care and love.

So the orphaned child was christened Nona (which, read backwards, is *anon*, short for 'anonymous' or 'unknown'), and Nona Browning she became. Sister Browning took her to Keswick in the Lake District, where she had bought a small cottage in the sunny Newlands Valley for her retirement. There she devoted her life to the little crippled child. She made the most extravagant plans for her. When she was old enough, she would have her legs and back straightened, and her poor feet put right. She would have her walking yet! And then would be the time for the hare-lip. Plastic surgeons could do wonders nowadays. She spoke her plans aloud as she tucked up the baby, and put her pram in a sunny corner of the garden. The child looked back at her with its dark eyes as if it understood every word; indeed, Mary Browning was quite sure that she did. She thought the world of the baby. There weren't many people, said she, who had a child with a nature as sweet and good-tempered as Nona's. She almost forgot about the baby's twisted limbs and disfigured lip, until some stranger would peep into the pram and turn away with a shudder of disgust.

All went well for a time and Mary Browning was very happy. But, alas, her dreams for her adopted child were never to be fulfilled – as far as she was concerned. One morning the neighbours, wakened by the unusual sound of the baby crying, broke into the cottage to find Mary lying dead in bed.

And now it was a question of what best to do for the doubly orphaned child. She was taken to the local hospital, where she was looked after and petted by everybody, from the Matron down to the youngest ward-maid. They all adored her, ugly and misshapen though she was. As she grew older she began to crawl like any ordinary baby, though it was obvious that she would, as things were, never walk upright. The orthopaedic surgeon, newly come from a London hospital, had not yet acquired that detachment which comes with age and experience. He looked down at the dark-eyed child as she squirmed along the passages, in and out of the wards, looking so like a frog that the patients laughed at her through their tears, and he thought: 'What a responsibility rests with me! Just to think that I, with the skill that God has given me, may re-form those twisted limbs, so that this poor scrap of humanity will one day stand upright and walk, instead of creeping on the ground like an animal!' His heart overflowed with pity for the child, for, even if she were to walk and run about like other children, she never could be *quite* like other children. There was still the disfigurement to her lip, and if that were to be cured, medical science could not completely mend the cleft palate. Her speech would remain blurred. Well, it was up to him to do what he could for her, and he felt a surge of exultation to think that *his* hands would perform the miracle.

There followed years of pain, and frustration, and occasional triumph. Months when Nona lay with her legs encased in plaster, suspended with pulleys, or weighted with irons. But after each operation, she improved. The helpless feet, once turned out sideways like frogs' feet, were now straight, and lay in front of her, side by side, like pieces of ivory – tiny feet, exquisitely formed. In fact, her whole small body, now that the surgeon had finished with it, was exquisite, the legs long and slender, the head beautifully set on her shoulders, her small-boned hands lying on the counterpane of her cot like pale pink shells. Doctors and nurses looked down at her, puzzled. It was quite obvious that she could now walk – if only she would. The trouble was, she didn't seem to want to. She refused to make the effort. Patients from other parts of the hospital came into the Children's Ward and talked to her by the hour; they hung toys on the end of the cot to attract her, hoping that she would pull herself up in an effort to reach them, but she never did. The Matron, a delicate sweet-faced woman, used to tiptoe into the ward and sit beside the child, willing her to walk, but all to no avail. Nona seemed to be quite content to lie there peacefully. It was as if she said: 'I have endured so much; I am so very tired. Please let me rest.'

Nona Browning became the hospital mascot. No visitor came who did not look in to see her. The Children's Ward was filled with flowers and toys that had been brought for her. They called her the Sleeping Beauty, since it looked as if only the kiss of a fairy prince would bring her fully to life.

When she was five years old, the young surgeon made a decision.

'I've done all I can for her,' he declared to his colleagues, 'and you, I am sure, have done all *you* can. I have ideas of sending her to London – to the new Thames Street Children's Hospital, to see if, perhaps, they can succeed where we have failed. They have all the latest orthopaedic equipment, and a very brilliant surgeon – a young man called Rounthwaite. Matter of fact, he comes from this part of the world – North of England, anyway. His home is in Newcastle, I believe. I'd like him to see her.'

Chapter 2

The Children's Hospital

Later that summer, Nona was sent by ambulance to Windermere, where she was placed carefully on the seat of a first-class compartment of the London train. A nurse accompanied her. At Waterloo another ambulance was waiting, and she was carried to it, under the curious gaze of a crowd of onlookers who had gathered to see what it was all about. From there she was whisked off to the Hospital for Sick Children in Thames Street.

In this famous hospital was every modern device to help spastic and incapacitated children. A swimming-pool of warmed salt water in which they could exercise their weak or distorted limbs with the least possible effort, and all the latest equipment to encourage the cripples not only to walk, but to run and climb. And wonderful it was to see the things they could do! I would like to be able to say that Nona Browning got up from her crib and began to walk and run about, but I cannot. The Thames Street hospital had no more success than the Keswick one. The child allowed the physiotherapist to examine her and exercise her limbs; she lay passively in the water in a harness, and did whatever she was told, but it seemed that nothing would make her pull herself upright and stand of her own free will, let alone walk. And then, when hope had almost vanished, came that day I spoke of at the beginning of my story.

It happened like this. Mr Rounthwaite, the brilliant young orthopaedic surgeon, had married early in his career, and his wife happened to be a ballet dancer. She was a member of the Royal Ballet, and danced under her maiden name of Sylvia Swan. At Christmas, the Thames Street hospital (like all hospitals) spared no pains to entertain the patients under its roof. The fun began on Christmas Eve with a party of carol singers from the nearby church, and ended on Christmas Night with Father Christmas bearing a sack of presents – one for every child. In between, was a non-stop entertainment. Dick Whittington arrived straight from Drury Lane with his cat, a large furry beast that purred, and rubbed itself gently against the legs of the children. It meowed and rolled golden eyes beside the beds of those who were strapped to pulleys, or lay on their tummies, or flat on their backs. One little boy recovering from polio, who had been unable to breathe without oxygen apparatus, forgot about it and found himself breathing quite naturally – to his own great astonishment, and to the gratification of the doctors who had been hoping this would happen long ago. In the same way they hoped that Nona Browning would at least sit up to watch the fun, but she lay still in her bed, making no effort at all.

After Dick Whittington and his cat had disappeared through the swing doors at the end of the long ward where the entertainment was being held, there was a short pause. Then in came Cinderella and her coach, drawn by twelve white mice (children from a local dancing school dressed in grey tights, with mouses' heads and long tails). They raced scampering over the polished floor, to an accompaniment of delighted squeals from the watching children as they pretended to nibble the legs of tiny Georgie Smith, the youngest patient in the ward.

After Cinderella and her coach had gone, nurses appeared with a wonderful tea. Trolleys were wheeled in, laden with plates of quivering jellies, baskets of fruit, trifles, and mountains of sandwiches and cakes and sausages on sticks.

There was ice-cream, too, and lemonade, and crackers with gifts inside, and a huge Christmas cake made of sponge with marshmallow filling and pink icing-sugar reindeers romping round the sides. On top was a sugar Father Christmas, with a long beard of white cotton wool and a sack of chocolates on his back.

And then, when the children could eat no more, the trolleys were wheeled out, the swing doors opened again, and in danced the most beautiful Sugar Plum Fairy you ever saw! Sylvia Swan was a dancer who gave of her best no matter what the occasion was. Some dancers from a company as exalted as the Royal Ballet might have considered a party for crippled children a little beneath them, but not Sylvia. Her husband thought he had never seen her dance more lightly or more crisply. The specially taped music fell upon the air like bits of ice dropping into a pool. You could have heard a pin drop in the ward. And then came the wonderful *pas de deux*. Tchaikovsky's surging music rose in a crescendo as the dancer's partner lifted her high in the air. This young man was Toni Rossini, the choreographer, and he did not usually partner Sylvia. She generally danced with the famous Josef Linsk, but when she had told Josef of her offer to dance for the sick children on Christmas Day, he had flatly refused to partner her.

'My dear Sylvia,' he had said, 'I'd do anything for you, but dance at a children's party – and on Christmas Day, of all days! – no, no! I am not a Santa Claus, nor a conjurer!' So Sylvia had enlisted Toni's help, and he had readily agreed to dance with her.

She found herself being glad that it was Rossini, and not Linsk, who was partnering her on this occasion. Toni was so very unselfish; whereas Josef *was* just a little inclined to show off. Once or twice he had been thinking so much about his own brilliant turns that he had almost let her fall. In the male *solo*, of course, Toni couldn't touch Josef, whose brilliance almost made one blink as he leapt high into the air with his flickering *grand batterie*. But there was something about Toni that captivated the children. They clapped their little hands and cheered when he had finished.

And then the miracle happened! Sylvia began the famous *solo*, and Nona Browning, who until this moment had lain so still in her bed that everyone had forgotten about her, stretched out her hands towards the dancer. Her tiny fingers closed round the rail at the head of her bed and slowly, slowly (while the Sugar Plum Fairy flung out her arms in lovely *ports de bras*) the child sat up. And now the nurses and doctors had seen what was happening, and they held their breath as she stood upright and walked with faltering steps to the end of the bed, where she stood, her great dark eyes fixed upon the lovely dancer, who didn't yet know that her art had achieved what all the wonders of medical science had been striving to do for the last two years.

The *solo* ended, and Sylvia found that the limelight usually accorded to a *ballerina* had switched over to the bedside of a crippled child. Fortunately Sylvia was a modest girl, and when she found out what had happened, she went over to Nona's bedside and talked to her.

'You liked my dancing?' she said. 'I'm so glad!'

Nona put out a tiny hand and said something which the nurse translated. (The nurses could all understand the child's slurred speech by now.) 'She says she wants to dance like you.'

Sylvia put her arms round the little girl.

'And so you shall, my darling! You'll learn to walk for me, won't you? Then I shall teach you to dance. Shall I come back tomorrow?'

Nona nodded, her eyes shining like stars.

'Oh, Sylvia – perhaps you shouldn't have promised that!' Her young husband had come over to her and was standing looking down at them. He limped slightly, and perhaps it

17

was his own disability that accounted for his amazing success with children. 'She'll be terribly disappointed when you can't come.'

'But, my dear – I *shall* come,' said Sylvia. 'Even if I have to cut my practice for half an hour, I shall come. I can always finish off my centre-practice *here*!' She laughed merrily. 'We'll have the nurses turning into ballet dancers next! Seriously, though, if it's true that I've helped this poor child today, and can go on helping her, I feel more thrilled than I've ever been with all my curtain calls and bouquets at Covent Garden!' It was true. Sylvia felt that Nona had given her a bouquet more lovely than all the flowers she had received from her many admirers.

Chapter 3

Convalescence

The next day Sylvia returned, and the day after that, and the day after that. Nona improved so fast that soon she was walking – at first hesitantly, and then confidently. At the end of three months, she was beginning to play with the other children. It wasn't long before the hospital authorities decided that it was time for her to go back to the North of England, so as to make room for another patient. In the fresh air of Keswick, they said, she could complete her convalescence under the care of Mr Calthrop, the young surgeon who had operated upon her in the first place. Miss Swan (whose dancing had been the cause of the child's miraculous recovery) offered to accompany her, as she herself was travelling up to Newcastle for a short visit to her husband's mother. She was only too glad, she said, to go round by Keswick and look after Nona. After that, she was going abroad with the Company.

'I shall only be gone for a couple of months,' she told Nona, 'and when I come back, I expect you'll be dancing as well as me!'

She was joking, of course, and had she known that the child would take her seriously, she would have been very upset, for, even if her limbs became quite normal, how could a child with such a disfigurement to her face ever become a dancer? It's a fact that often too much emphasis is put upon the part physical beauty plays in a dancer's career; it's also a fact that few dancers of the first rank can be called strictly beautiful in the accepted sense of the word, but there are some things that no dancer could ever surmount – a pronounced squint, for instance, or, as in Nona's case, a hare-lip.

And so Nona returned to the little Lakeland hospital, walking like any other little girl, and by her side walked the beautiful ballerina, Sylvia Swan. No wonder it caused a stir in the town! The wide verandas of the hospital had been thrown open to the sun, for it was now May, one of the loveliest of months in the Lake District. The great mountain, Skiddaw, brooded over the little town, sheltering it from the cold north winds; the hills of Borrowdale shimmered in a blue heat-haze, and Derwentwater shone like a silver shield.

'Oh, what a beautiful place!' cried Sylvia with a catch of her breath, when they walked down from the little station, leaving instructions for Nona's luggage to be sent on. 'Although I know it well, I get a shock of pleasure every time I come back. Aren't you lucky, Nona, to be able to stay here until you are quite well?'

The child looked up at Sylvia, her dark eyes troubled. Of *course* she was glad to be coming back to the hospital where everyone had been so kind to her, of *course* it was lovely to be able to walk about like other children, but . . .

'You *will* come back, Miss Swan?' she whispered. 'I couldn't bear it if you didn't.'

'Of course I will,' said Sylvia. 'You have my promise.'

Since it was impossible, either by train or bus, to get over to Newcastle that same night, Sylvia stayed the night in Keswick. That evening (at the request of the staff), she went to the hospital to entertain the patients.

'I'm sorry I can't dance for you,' she said apologetically, 'but I'm not allowed to, you know, without permission, and in any case I haven't any ballet shoes or a costume to dance in, but I'll show you a little classical *mime*, if you like. Then, perhaps, when you go to see *Swan Lake* or any of the other classical ballets, you will enjoy them more.' She went on to explain how classical *mime* (unlike free *mime*) is completely 'set'. That is to say, one particular gesture means 'yes', another 'no', and these gestures must always be done in exactly the same way, and can never mean anything else. She showed the fascinated patients how you could 'talk' in *mime*; how Odette, the Swan Princess, tells the Prince of her enchantment; how she has been changed into a swan (shown by a lovely 'flying' movement of the arms); how she can only be freed from the spell by the promise of someone to love and to marry her (pointing to her ring finger). Then she took the part of the Prince, and showed them how he tells Odette he has fallen in love with her beauty, and will marry her, and so disenchant her – all this without a word spoken.

The watching patients and nurses were amazed and touched to see how little Nona Browning followed the gestures of the ballerina, trying her best to copy them.

'If you ask me, I think she's under a spell herself, poor mite,' one of them said, 'but it will take more than a fairy prince to cure her of her cruel disability, I'm thinking!'

The months that followed her return to Keswick were happy ones for Nona – some of the happiest of her life. She played in the open verandas when it was wet and went out into the garden surrounding the hospital when it was fine. People visiting relatives or friends heard about the 'wonder child' as she had been nicknamed, and they offered to take her out with them, sometimes in their cars, sometimes on the lake in a boat, or on one of the launches that ply busily backwards and forwards, from shore to shore during the summer season. Sometimes they walked in the woods or had picnics, or sat high above the lake on the mossy Old Road that clings to the mountainside beneath Cat Bells.

The summer wore on. Sylvia returned from her tour abroad, and, true to her promise, paid another short visit to Keswick. She found Nona a changed child – sunburnt and laughing, with straight limbs and a lovely graceful way of walking. Her dark hair and eyes shone with life, until you almost forgot about her disfigurement and thought her pretty.

'Do the *mime* scene from *Swan Lake* for me, please Miss Swan,' begged Nona. They were sitting on a stretch of turf, half-way up Latrigg. 'Please, please, Miss Swan.'

So Sylvia good-naturedly did it for her, to the great astonishment of a party of hikers who had appeared on the pathway ahead.

'Oh, thank you,' said Nona. 'And now will you do the part of the Prince when he tells Odette he loves her.'

Sylvia blushed. The hikers (several of whom were young men) were looking at her in amusement. 'I think we'd better leave it till next time, Nona, dear,' she said. 'Everyone might not understand what it is we are doing.'

'There might never be a next time,' said Nona with an insight far beyond her years.

'Oh, don't look on the black side,' laughed Sylvia. All the same, she shivered as if a cloud had passed over the sun, and although the lake shone as blue as ever, she felt that some of its brightness had dimmed. What, she wondered, would become of this unfortunate, sensitive, intelligent little girl, with her tragic, disfigured face?

August came, and with it the news that Nona was to be sent to a Special School in Newcastle, where she would be taught to speak more clearly than she did at the moment. She would attend this school during the daytime, but would live in an orphanage nearby.

There were many tears when the time came for her to say good-bye to the kind nurses and all her friends, but of course it was impossible for her to stay in the little hospital any longer, for she was now, as far as the doctors were concerned, quite well. She was six years old, and her limbs almost as straight as other children's – straighter than some. Only one shoulder remained a little higher than the other, and sometimes when she was tired she limped slightly.

Chapter 4

The Orphanage

On a windy corner of Elswick Road, Newcastle-upon-Tyne, where the mean streets tumble down to the Tyne like crazy ladders, stood the Fenwick Foundation Home for Orphaned Children. It was an old, yellow-brick building of extreme ugliness. The windows of its chilly basements were protected from stone-throwing by iron grilles which kept out the sun as effectively as they kept out stones and unwelcome intruders, so that there was always a pale glimmer of electric light down there, even in the middle of the day.

The front windows looked out over the main road, with its continuous roar of traffic – buses, lorries, and commercial vehicles of every shape and size, besides the usual stream of private cars. The back windows saw a sea of grey roofs, with underneath a network of back-yards. Only up in the attics could you catch a glimpse of the river far below, with a haze of green trees and meadows beyond. On a fine day you might be lucky enough to catch a glimpse of blue hills. Here Nona used to sit warming herself in a shaft of sunlight, and dreaming of the mountains of her beloved Lakeland. Below – so far down that they looked like mere specks – the children played and fought on the steep slope of Rye Hill. Their screams and shouts of laughter floated up to her, but she did not hear them. She was hearing in her imagination the roar of the Lakeland waterfalls, and the cry of seagulls as they circled over Friar's

Crag, as the launch passed by on its way up Derwentwater to the Barrow Landing.

It wasn't the cold and gloomy house, with its echoing passages and barred windows, that made Nona Browning one of the unhappiest little girls in all Newcastle. It wasn't that she was treated unkindly by the staff of the orphanage either. Indeed, she was a general favourite with those in authority because of her gentle ways, and her obvious desire to please. Miss Barnes (the principal) tried her best not to discriminate between the children, and Miss Humphreys the secretary and other officials did likewise, but there was something about Nona that aroused their pity so that unconsciously they found themselves taking her part against the other children.

Yes, it was the other children that made Nona's life a misery. Children, like animals, can be very cruel to any one of their kind that is 'different' from the rest, and Nona was certainly different, both physically and mentally. When any member of the staff was in sight, the children dare not openly bully her, but in the dormitories at night, after Miss Barnes had paid her good night visit and disappeared downstairs to her own quarters to watch the television, they tormented her like matadors baiting a bull – only in this case the bull was a gentle, defenceless child. They made fun of her slurred speech, and mimicked the way she walked with one shoulder slightly higher than the other. It wasn't only in the dormitories that it happened, but out in the playground too. The children followed her wherever she went, making rude noises and giving her sly pokes and pinches when she tried to pass them. Tommy Bates was the worst. He was a tall, handsome lad of ten (though he looked about twelve), with black curly hair, and a big coarse mouth. When Nona wanted to escape her tormentors and go out into the strip of sooty garden that lay beyond the asphalt playground, there was Tommy barring her way.

'You gotta ask me nicely,' he would tell her. 'Go on – down on your knees!'

Poor Nona would have to kneel down on the muddy ground before he would let her pass, and even then she knew that he would give her a sly kick on the way. Sometimes her courage failed her, and she would turn tail and run away – or try to – but usually Tommy put out a long arm and hauled her back.

'Cowardy custard! Cowardy custard!' he would yell, and all the other children joined in.

'Nona Browning's a cowardy custard! Nona Browning's a cowardy custard!'

'Now then,' Tommy would say, holding the cringing child fast, 'down on yer knees and say after me: "please can I go into the garden, Tommy, dear?"'

'Pleeth can I go into the garthen, Tommy, deeth,' repeated Nona.

'Louder!'

Usually she had to repeat the words many times before he was satisfied, and after each repetition the other children stood round in a ring, mocking her . . . 'Nona Browning canna say "please", she says, "pleeth". Nona Browning canna say "garden", she says "garthen"!'

No wonder Nona was as miserable a scrap of humanity as you could find anywhere. Her speech became more blurred as her mental agony increased, until it was almost impossible to understand a word she said; the droop of her right shoulder, hardly perceptible when she had left the Keswick hospital, became more and more noticeable.

The orphanage was run on 'family' lines, with the children divided into small groups under the care of a housemother. Each family had a territory of its own consisting of a dormitory which the girls of the family shared with the girls of another family. Likewise the boys shared with the boys of another group. The Authorities realized that this was not a perfect arrangement, but it was the best that could be done under the circumstances. Each housemother had a bedroom of her own, and there was a sitting-room which was shared by the whole family. In this way the children got a taste of family life. There was a communal dining-hall – a large gloomy room in the basement, smelling of cabbage and carbolic soap. The dark brown linoleum on the floor was so highly polished by a succession of orphans who, having reached the ripe age of twelve, were considered old enough to lend a hand in the running of the orphanage, that it always looked wet. The walls had been painted a bright pink by some optimistic soul who had thought to bring a bit of cheerfulness into the place.

Nona hated the meals there, not because of the gloom or the smells, but because her table manners were rather better than the other children's, owing to her having lived so long in hospitals.

'Oh, look at Nona Browning! She doesn't half think she's somebody! . . . Nona Browning never eats peas with a knife. *Never*! . . . Please *pars* the salt . . . Nona Browning wants some war-tar. Nona Browning never says watter . . . Pars a glass of war-tar to Nona Browning! . . . Nona Browning wants some war-tar!'

At her school, which was for children with special needs, Nona was happy. They say that 'a fellow feeling makes us wondrous kind', and it was certainly true in her case. All the children there had problems – of hearing, sight or speech – and they warmly supported one another. Nona was taught how to speak more intelligibly, and how to make herself understood by other means than mere speech – for instance, that to hold out a hand when you say 'how do you do?' makes the words plainer than the gesture alone. It reminded her of the classical *mime* gestures Miss Swan had taught her. The Mayfield School was housed in an old mansion on the edge of the city, and it was surrounded by parkland. Nona went there by bus every morning, as it was a day school only. Every night she walked back to the orphanage with dragging feet, feeling physically sick at the thought of meeting Tommy Bates and his cronies. If it hadn't been for her housemother, a Mrs Makepeace, whom she loved dearly, she would have run away.

Mrs Makepeace had lost her husband some years ago, and her children had all grown up and married, so she was filling the gap in her life by looking after other people's less fortunate children – a good work if ever there was one. Gladys Makepeace often wondered why little Nona Browning looked so sad and frightened, but so careful were Tommy Bates and the other bullies to carry on their activities in secret that she never suspected the truth.

And then one day something happened that changed Nona's unhappy existence, and gave her some peace. A new child arrived at the orphanage, a boy of about ten. He had run away from home because (so he said) his parents didn't want him. For weeks he had roamed the streets, sleeping under bridges, in warehouses, or in the narrow alleyways that honeycomb the old tumbledown wall that once surrounded the city. He had kept himself alive by eating out of garbage bins, or picking up crusts of bread thrown out to the birds. Finally he had been picked up by the police and taken to the Station to be questioned, although as far as they could make out, he had stolen nothing; nor had he done anything wrong. They found out, in fact, that his story was perfectly true – his parents *didn't* want him. Neither of them seemed to care in the least what became of their young son. The father declared frankly that he 'couldn't care less', and the mother that she 'could do nothing with him'.

So the boy, whose name was Jude Dockerty, came to live in the big house at the corner of Elswick Road, where he was given a suit of clothes to replace his rags, and the first square meal he had ever eaten. He was put into the Makepeace family, where there happened to be a vacancy.

One day when Nona came home from school about a week after Jude had arrived at the orphanage, she found a magazine lying open on the sitting-room table. Mrs Makepeace had been called to answer the telephone, so Nona sat there looking at it. She did not turn the pages because it wasn't her magazine, but she couldn't help seeing the picture on the open page. It was of three dancers in long floating ballet dresses grouped round a young man in classical costume. Underneath the picture were the words: 'Weston, Rosetti, Swan and Linsk in the famous group from the ballet *Les Sylphides*.'

'Mrs Makepeace! Oh, Mrs Makepeace!' gasped Nona when her housemother came back into the room. 'Look what it says here – it says "Swan". That must be *my* Miss Swan!'

Gladys Makepeace loved the ballet, it was her one passion. She was nearly as excited as Nona when she discovered that her 'little dumb foundling' (as she thought of Nona) knew the beautiful ballerina.

'Sylvia Swan?' she said. 'You really mean to say you know her?'

'Of course I do. She came to my hospital – the one in London, and she was a beautiful Sugar Plum Fairy in a ballet. Miss Swan told me the story. It's called *The Nutcracker*, and it's about a little girl called Clara, only Clara had a mummy and a daddy and lots of friends, and she was a very pretty little girl – not ugly like me.'

'Oh, my darling! My darling!' cried Gladys Makepeace, putting her arms round Nona. But Nona was obviously lost in the story, and wasn't feeling sorry for herself at all. 'A fairy prince came to Clara and took her away to fairyland,' she went on. 'First they went to the Land of Sweets, and while she was there, all the fairies came and danced for her. And that's where my Miss Swan was the Sugar Plum Fairy,' she ended triumphantly. Most people wouldn't have been able to make much of the child's excited gabble, but Gladys Makepeace understood every word.

'Well fancy that!' she said.

'And Miss Swan taught me how to dance,' said Nona. 'Like *this*. It's called *mime*, and it all means something. This,' (she described a circle round her face with one hand) 'this means "I think you are very beautiful". It's what the Prince says when he first sees the enchanted Princess in a ballet called *Swan Lake*.'

Gladys Makepeace watched her compassionately. The poor mite! With her affliction it wasn't likely that anyone (let alone a prince) would say these words to her – not even in *mime*! Long years afterwards, when she saw pictures of the beautiful Nona Browning, she would recall this moment.

'Well, I'll tell you something,' she said at length, 'the Royal Ballet is coming to the Theatre Royal next week. Would you like to go with me, Nona? I intended to take one of you, and it seems to me that you'll appreciate it more than any of the others.'

'Oh, Mrs Makepeace, do you really mean it?' cried Nona. 'I can't believe it! You mean that my Miss Swan will be there?'

'Now I can't promise that,' said Gladys Makepeace, 'for I don't know yet. Nobody knows until the programme is published. It will probably be only the junior members of the company – it's not very often, if ever, that we get the stars up here. But cheer up!' (Nona's face had fallen with disappointment) 'they're sure to have one or two of their best dancers to "stiffen" the rest, and Sylvia Swan may very well be one of them. It's quite likely, after all, as they must know she came from Newcastle. Oh, yes! She used to live in Cogg's Road, not so very far from here.'

While Nona and Mrs Makepeace had been talking, the other children had been arriving back from their state school, which was just round the corner, but which finished later than Nona's. Tommy Bates was taking it all in, and scheming in his wicked mind how he would bait Nona. 'Bally, indeed!' He'd give her ballet!

After tea, when they were sent out into the playground, he accosted her, after taking a furtive look round to see if Mrs Makepeace or any other members of the staff were in sight. The coast was clear, so he caught the child by the arm.

'Goin' to the bally, are yer?' he said, twisting it behind her back. 'My! Aren't we gettin' stuck-up! Rock music ain't good enough fer Nona Browning. She 'as to 'ave bally. "I think you are ver-ee bu-tee-ful! My lover-ly Sylvia Swan!" ' He imitated Nona's *mime* gestures, making a hideous mockery of them.

He certainly wasn't expecting what happened next. Nona, the meek, half-witted child (or so he thought her) flew at him in a fury. She wouldn't stand up for herself, but when it was her beloved Miss Swan who was attacked, it was quite another matter.

'How dare you! What do you know about ballet, anyhow? What do you know of Miss Swan? How dare you make fun of her!'

'I dare do *anything*!' boasted Tommy, drawing himself up to his full height, which was head and shoulders above Nona. 'And right now I'm going to teach you to show a little respect for your betters.' He seized Nona's thin arm again and gave it another painful twist, forcing her to her knees. 'Now you say as you're sorry for what you've done. Go on now!'

'I haven't done anything,' whispered Nona.

'Ho! You ain't done nothin', ain't you? Well, for a start you attacked *me*. Didn't she?' He appealed to the ring of expectant children who had closed round them to see the fun.

'Ya! Ya!' they shouted. 'Give it 'er, Tommy!'

And then, just as Tommy was making up his mind whether to go on twisting the victim's arm (a technique he had brought to a fine art during the ten years of his bullying life), or to administer a kick which would send her sprawling face downwards in the mud, a diversion was caused by the new boy, Jude Dockerty, who had appeared at the back of the crowd and demanded to know what all the excitement was about.

'I'm just about to teach young Nona Browning not to be cheeky,' said Tommy with a hideous grin.

'Not while I'm here you aren't,' said Jude. 'You leave the kid alone.'

'Oo says so?' demanded Tommy.

'I do.'

'And oo's goin' to make us leave 'er alone if I dunna want to?' said Tommy.

'*I* am.'

There was a rustle and a murmur amongst the crowd of children. They sensed a fight. The newcomer was an unknown quantity, but everyone could see that he was smaller and lighter by far than Tommy Bates. They didn't think much of his chances. Why, Tommy would swallow him alive!

'Ya!' they shouted. 'Give it 'im, Tommy! Let 'im 'ave it!'

By this time Jude had forced his way through the crowd of children, and Tommy lunged at him. But something went wrong. Tommy's fist hit the empty air – where Jude's face had been a few seconds ago – and he all but lost his balance. The next minute a foot hooked itself round his ankle, and he went sprawling in the mud.

'Ya!' yelled the crowd half-heartedly. They always

believed in supporting the winning side (Tommy, up to now), but at the moment it looked as if Tommy's star was waning. Not for nothing had young Jude Dockerty made the city streets his home during the greater part of his ten years. He had learned early to defend himself, or he would never have survived the attacks made on him by the gangs of older children who had tried to bully him or make him join up with them. His fighting technique he had gleaned from various sources – a sailor, whose ship was laid up in the Tyne for repairs, had taught him a smattering of judo; a newspaper man who had once been a champion boxer, had taught him the elements of that sport. Experience had done the rest. It was a good thing that Jude was at heart a decent lad, or he might well have become a menace to society.

But now Tommy Bates was on his feet again, and preparing to lay low his opponent. The result was the same as before, only this time Tommy didn't get up. He lay there on the ground blinking up at his vanquisher, and looking dazed with surprise and shock.

'You just let me know when you've had enough,' said Jude nonchalantly, while the ring of children shuffled their feet uneasily. They were quite sure by this time that they were on the wrong side, and were wondering how to change over without losing face.

As for Nona, her dark eyes were shining with gratitude and admiration. From that day she worshipped the ground Jude walked on. Not that he took much notice of her – he was of an age when little girls didn't appeal, but he saw that she wasn't bullied. The other children, once deprived of the leadership of the bully, Tommy Bates, found that Nona was kind and gentle, and they became quite fond of her. They didn't even tease her about her passion for the ballet.

Chapter 5

Backstage

Mrs Makepeace had managed to book seats for herself and Nona at the Theatre Royal for an evening performance. So, on the following Monday night, they settled themselves in the middle of the third row of the upper circle, with a programme between them, and a small box of chocolates on Nona's knee. Gladys Makepeace was making sure it would be an evening Nona would remember all her life.

'Oh, Mrs Makepeace, can I look inside quickly?' cried Nona. Unlike most children her thoughts were all for the programme – she had quite forgotten the box of chocolates. 'Please, Mrs Makepeace, may I look?'

'Of course look inside,' said her housemother in amusement. She only half believed Nona's story about Miss Swan, but if it kept her happy . . . 'Be quick, before the lights go down!'

Nona opened the programme and quickly scanned the list of dancers. Her face fell, and she looked up with tragic dark eyes. 'She isn't here! Oh, Mrs Makepeace, how shall I bear it?'

A small slip of paper had fallen unheeded to the floor between their two seats. Gladys picked it up. 'What's this?' she said, passing it to Nona. 'I haven't my glasses on, but it looks to me like an *errata* notice. You read what it says.'

Nona took it apathetically. Then her face changed, and she almost jumped out of her seat in her excitement. 'She *is* dancing, Mrs Makepeace! It says here: "The rôle of Odette from *Swan Lake* will be danced by Sylvia Swan,

34

and not Belinda Beaucaire as stated in the programme."
Oh, how wonderful! I remember Miss Swan telling me that
Odette was her favourite rôle. It's after the First Interval.
How shall I ever wait?'

Mrs Makepeace listened to Nona's chatter, amazed at
her knowledge of the ballet. Just imagine – the child called
a dance a *solo*! And now she was talking of '*pas de deux*',
and '*divertissements*' . . .

'They're the dances that don't have anything to do with
the story of the ballet. I mean you could take them out of
one ballet and put them in another, and it wouldn't matter
a bit. Miss Swan told me about them. They're usually done
in front of some very important person, like a king and
queen, or a duke, or a prince. They're doing some tonight
from *Le Casse Noisette*. That will be after the Snowflake scene. Chocolat (Danse Espagnole); Café (Danse
Arabe); Thé (Danse Chinois); Bouffon (Danse des
Mirlitons) . . . Oh, I can't believe it – they're doing the
Grand Pas De Deux too, and the Dance of the Sugar Plum
Fairy. It's the first dance I ever saw my Miss Swan do. I
don't believe this other person, Belinda Beaucaire, will be
half as good as my Miss Swan.'

She chattered on and on, until suddenly there was a burst
of clapping for the conductor of the symphony orchestra,
who had just appeared. Then the lights went down, and
the performance had begun.

The first half of the programme was taken up by a ballet
called *The Carnival of Animals*, with music by Saint Saëns.
You could tell by the music which animal it was supposed
to be, even if you hadn't seen Vicki Scott as The Gentleman
with Long Ears (the Donkey) or Ella Rosetti's lovely tran-
quil Swan, or Rosanna Corelli's Cuckoo in The Forest.

Although Nona hadn't expected to enjoy this ballet, or
any ballet that her beloved Miss Swan wasn't in, for that
matter, she found herself loving every minute of it, though

35

she couldn't help exclaiming when the curtain rose on *Le Casse Noisette* and she saw the Dance of the Sugar Plum Fairy: 'Oh, she's not *half* as good as my Miss Swan!' She enjoyed the performance just the same, however.

And then came the moment that Nona was waiting for – the Odette solo from the ballet *Swan Lake*.

'Oh, she's even more beautiful than when she was the Sugar Plum Fairy!' she exclaimed, leaning forward in her seat so as to catch every movement. 'She's like a bird flying!'

At the end of the show, Gladys Makepeace took Nona backstage. Before climbing the long flights of stone stairs leading to the dressing-rooms, they went round to look at the stage. How different it was when one saw it from 'behind'! The lovely scenery of the Sleeping Beauty's garden could now be seen to be merely painted flats, while above their heads yawned the dusty flies, festooned with ropes like outsize spiderwebs.

'Oh, and look at the tree the cuckoo sat on!' cried Nona. 'Why, it's propped up with soap boxes!'

In one corner of the empty stage stood a small figure still wearing the costume of The Gentleman with Long Ears. She was talking to a Snowflake.

'Come *on*, Vicki! Whatever are you doing?' cried a voice from above them. Nona looked up and saw that a boy was looking down at them from far up in the flies. 'I thought you said you wanted to see how the limelights worked?'

'Well I do,' said The Gentleman with Long Ears without glancing up. 'Shan't be long!' She went on talking for a few minutes, then ran off, leaving the Snowflake standing by herself on the stage.

'Is the child really going up there?' asked Gladys Makepeace, staring at the place where the boy's head had appeared a moment ago. 'Is it safe?'

'Shouldn't think so!' laughed the Snowflake. 'But Vicki wouldn't care about that if she took it into her head to see how the limelights worked. Besides,' she added with a shrug, 'Jon's up there – he encourages her.'

'Is he a dancer?' asked Mrs Makepeace curiously.

'Not he! He's a stage designer. He's working with the company, and he was responsible for the backcloth of *Carnival of Animals*. It's rather good, don't you think? Incidentally, Jon is my brother, so perhaps I'm prejudiced!'

'How lucky you are to be in the Royal Ballet!' said Nona wistfully.

The Snowflake looked questioningly at Mrs Makepeace. 'What does she say?'

Then, when the elder woman had explained, the dancer asked: 'Does *she*' (indicating Nona) 'like ballet?'

'She's mad about it, poor lamb,' said Gladys. 'Seems she got to know one of the principals – a Miss Swan – when she was in hospital in London, and that started it.'

'Of, of course – Sylvia's husband is a doctor. Well, if you take my advice, kid,' (she turned to Nona) 'you'll steer clear of ballet. It's an awful lot of hard work, and an awful lot of disappointment too. You begin by having bright ideas of dancing Odette-Odile in *Lac*, or the Sugar Plum Fairy in *Nutcracker*, and end up (like me) as one of the back-row Swans (not even a cygnet as I'm too big!) or a Snowflake. Back row too! Eventually I expect I'll be a Court Lady or Giselle's Mother, and then *finis!*' She was joking, really, because everyone has to start by being in the *corps de ballet*. Margot Fonteyn's first rôle was a Snowflake in *Casse Noisette*, and as she herself puts it she 'hardly knew whether she was facing the audience or had her back to them!' This particular Snowflake, who was now giving Nona good advice, might end up by being a *prima ballerina*, or she might end her dancing days in the *corps de ballet* – one never knew!

'By the way,' continued the Snowflake, 'in case you're interested, my name is Felicity Craymore. My mother was a dancer – her name, before she married my father, was Stella Mason – but I don't think she liked a dancer's life very much. She tried her best to stop *me* from being one, and so did my father, but after a bit they saw I was quite decided, and they gave in. They're quite right, though – it's a dog's life!'

'I don't believe you really mean it,' said Nona.

Felicity laughed. She was beginning to understand Nona's queer way of speaking. 'Well, perhaps I don't. Or perhaps I'm like a silly moth, who knows quite well he's going to get burnt by the bright lights, but he goes on flying round them just the same. By the way, my mother is a friend of the one and only Veronica Weston. Now Veronica is exactly the right type for a dancer! She thinks of nothing but the ballet, and everything else has to take second place.' She gave a little sigh.

'You sound sad?' said Nona.

'I was just thinking of Vicki,' said Felicity. 'The girl who was here just now. You see Veronica Weston is Vicki's mother, and poor Vicki takes second place too! If Veronica Weston wasn't thinking so much about her own career, she'd notice that Vicki (wonderful dancer though she is) doesn't really care *that*' (she snapped her fingers) 'for dancing. We all know it – except her mother!'

'What about her father?' asked Nona.

'Her *father*! Have you met her father? No, of course you haven't. Do you know who *he* is? He's Sebastian Scott, the pianist and conductor. If anything, he's worse than Veronica! I mean he just sees *nothing*, except his own piano, and his own orchestra. The two of them get on famously together – one thinking of nothing but ballet; the other nothing but music. Neither of them notice that poor darling Vicki is there at all! Well, now that I've let off steam to someone, I'll admit that Veronica Weston is the sweetest

38

person alive, but there you are – she's a *prima ballerina*, and *prima ballerinas* aren't quite like other people, are they?'

'My Miss Swan is quite perfect,' declared Nona seriously.

Felicity burst into a peal of laughter.

'You *have* got a crush on her, haven't you!' she said. 'You're right – Sylvia Swan *isn't* quite as single-minded as Veronica Weston, but give her time! She isn't a *prima ballerina* yet – just a common-or-garden *ballerina*. There's a difference, you know. Sorry if I've offended you, but Sylvia Swan can't touch Weston as a dancer because nobody can.'

'Talking of Miss Swan,' put in Gladys Makepeace, 'I did promise Nona we'd pay her a visit in her dressing-room. The poor lamb would be so thrilled.' (She didn't add 'and so would I', which was the truth.) 'Do you think she'd mind – Miss Swan, I mean?'

'Not she,' said Felicity. 'She's very approachable. If you go down the passage over there, and up those steps, you'll come out on to the main staircase where the dressing-rooms are – the stars' dressing-rooms, I mean. The rest of us are up in the roof-tops – well, nearly! . . . Gosh! Look, there's Vicki!'

They all looked up, and beheld The Gentleman with Long Ears in the flies, her head, with its long donkey's ears, close to that of the boy, Jon Craymore. A spotlight sprang up and caught Nona and her two companions in its beam.

'Vicki, how dare you! You'll be shot!' cried Felicity. She turned to Nona and Mrs Makepeace. 'You'd better scoot. We'll be having the stage-manager round here at any moment to find out who's messing about with the lime-lights!'

Chapter 6

In Sylvia's Dressing-room

Sylvia Swan shared a star dressing-room with Ella Rosetti, one of the other principal dancers in the company. When she saw Nona, her face lit up.

'Ella, I want you to meet a little friend of mine,' she said to Miss Rosetti. 'You remember I told you all about Nona Browning, the little girl who saw me dance at Peter's hospital, and how she learned to walk. She made a marvellous recovery – well, you can see for yourself!' In actual fact, Sylvia was dismayed to see that Nona limped slightly when she walked, and that one shoulder was now noticeably higher than the other, but she was too much of a doctor's wife to show her feelings.

'Did you like the performance, Nona?' asked Ella Rosetti.

'I adored it,' answered Nona. 'I specially liked the bit in your ballet where the poor cuckoo asks why nobody loves her, and the Spirit of the Forest says: "*I* do!" You see, I understand all the bits with the *mime* in . . . *Why* – nobody – me – loves? . . . I – you – love.' She made the appropriate gestures in *mime* as she said the words, while the two dancers (and a dresser who had appeared in the doorway) watched her, fascinated.

'Wherever did she learn all that?' asked Ella. 'She does it very well.'

'Thanks for the unintentional compliment!' laughed Sylvia. '*I* taught her!'

At this moment a call-boy appeared, almost hidden by the

flowers he carried. 'Miss Rosetti! . . . Miss Swan! These are yours! Where d'you want 'em put?'

'Oh, anywhere, Jimmy, thank you,' said Sylvia. 'Ella and I won't quarrel about them! Who's that hiding behind those beautiful roses? Oh, Peter! Come in, Peter darling, and see who I've got here. You remember your little patient, Nona Browning?'

The young man looked down at the child, and his keen grey eyes saw what Sylvia's had seen – the drooping shoulder, but his words did not betray his thoughts.

'Why, of course I remember Nona. Well, Nona, how are you now?'

'I'm all right, thank you, Doctor,' said Nona. 'At least I am now that Jude – he's my friend – has stopped them making fun of me.'

Peter Rounthwaite's heart was full of pity. How cruel children could be! That anyone should taunt this poor child because of her disability was more than he could understand.

'Well, I'm glad you've got a protector, Nona,' he said.

'Oh, but Jude doesn't *protect* me!' laughed Nona. 'Most times he forgets all about me – he's so keen on football – but *they* (he knew she meant the other children) know he won't let them tease me.'

'I should think not!' said the young man. He turned suddenly to Sylvia, his lovely young wife. 'Do you know, my dear, I think Nona ought to have further treatment to strengthen her back and shoulders. I would suggest some elementary ballet lessons. She always seemed to be very interested in ballet, and the exercises will do her so much more good if she likes doing them.'

'You think the orphanage would agree to that?' asked Sylvia.

'Oh, I'm sure it could be arranged,' said the young surgeon. 'I'll see Dr Johnson about it.' (Dr Johnson was the orphanage doctor.) 'He's a friend of mine. I've known him for years. Once a week at that ballet school – what was it called – where you trained, would work wonders for the child.'

'You mean Mary Martin's?'

'Yes, that's the one. As I say, it would do her a world of good.'

Nona was listening, her dark eyes shining.

'You mean I can learn ballet?' she said breathlessly.

'Only the rudiments,' laughed Mr Rounthwaite (who, now that he was a surgeon, was a 'mister', and not a 'doctor'). 'I gather that you would like that?'

'Oh, I'd adore it!' cried Nona. 'I'll work so hard, Mr Rounthwaite, I'll be so happy – you can't imagine! Thank you, thank you!'

She almost danced out of the theatre by Gladys Makepeace's side.

At the stagedoor they found a crowd of fans waiting to see the stars come out, and on the steps stood Vicki Scott and Jon having a heated argument.

'You'd better come home with *me* to Bracken,' said Vicki. 'Perkins will drive us, and it's nearer than Broomyhough where your granny lives.'

But Jon shook his head.

'No, Granny will be expecting me. She'll wonder what's happened to me if I don't turn up.'

'My dear Jon – it'll be one o'clock in the morning by the time you get over there.'

'It's no good, Vicki – even if it's *two* o'clock, I must go tonight. I can let myself in without disturbing her, but I'll be there in the morning when she wakes up – that's the main thing. I promised her, you see, and Gran is very old – over ninety. I couldn't disappoint her.'

Vicki knew that when Jon had made up his mind, it was no use arguing with him. He was as 'obstinate as a cuddy', as they say in Northumberland! She gave a sigh of resignation. 'Oh, very well. If you must, I suppose you must. But what about tomorrow? It's my free day, and, if I remember rightly, yours too. Couldn't we meet somewhere and have a picnic? What do you say to riding over to that old peel-house on the moors above Garside – you know the one I mean? It's about half-way between Bracken and Broomyhough. You could borrow a mount from the Robsons at the farm.'

'That suits me,' said Jon with alacrity. He didn't flatter himself that he had any attraction for Vicki. She was merely lonely and she considered him better than no one – that was all! He, on his part, was very fond of her, and he snatched any opportunity that would mean seeing more of her. All of which goes to show that young Jon showed considerable strength of character, when he refused to spend the night at Bracken, Vicki's home, simply and solely to keep his promise to his old great-grand-parent.

'That suits me,' he answered. 'What time?'

'Oh, twelvish,' said Vicki. 'Then I needn't get up at crack of dawn.'

So saying, she turned her back upon him, and went in search of Perkins and the car, while Jon set off for the garage where he had left his little sports car.

Chapter 7

Jon and Vicki

Vicki reached the old Northumbrian peel-house before Jon. She had said 'it's half-way', but she had left poor Jon with the bigger half! She led her pony into the bottom part of the old building and tethered him to a ring in the wall. It was very dark owing to the fact that there were no windows, and the only light there was came in from the low massive door. There was a pile of sweet-smelling hay in one corner, so she pulled out an armful and gave it to the pony.

'There you are, Maestro,' she said. 'I'll have to remember to tell John Dodd I pinched it. I'm sure he won't mind.'

She went out into the spring sunshine, and looked around her. No Jon in sight yet, so she walked up the sheep track that led over the shoulder of the nearest hill, and looked down into a hollow formed by an outcrop of rock. Here lay one of those tiny mountain tarns that one finds in unexpected places on the Northumbrian moors. The wind ruffled its surface, so that one minute it was dark blue, and the next shining silver. Wild duck rose honking from the reeds nearby, and a pair of grouse raised the echoes with their metallic clatter of wings.

Vicki had seen the tarn many times before – in the winter when ice crackled along its edges; in the summer time when its still waters lay quivering in the heat. She had once bathed in it in October, when the summer's sun had warmed its waters, but she had never been here in the spring. There was a drift of white along its southern bank that intrigued her. Surely it couldn't be snow in June! But she found, when she scrambled down the steep hillside to investigate, that it was.

And then she saw something bright and alive floating on the water on the far side of the tarn. It was a large tortoise-shell butterfly that had fallen in and was now helplessly bogged down by its own bright outspread wings.

'Oh, you poor thing!' cried Vicki. She dashed to the rescue, slipping and sliding on the rocky slabs at the edge of the tarn. The butterfly was drifting further out into the middle of the pool, and she found that it was already out of her reach. She looked round for a dead branch and, having found one, tried to get the insect on to it.

'Oh, you silly, stupid insect!' she cried in exasperation, as the butterfly made no attempt to crawl on to the branch. 'Can't you see I'm trying to help you!' And then a gust of wind rushed over the brow of the hill, hit the water with a slap, sending ripples and waves from shore to shore and carrying the butterfly still further out. Vicki, trying in a last vain endeavour to make her arm even longer, overbalanced and fell flat in the water.

She wasn't a strong swimmer ('once across the pool is about my limit' she had once said at school), and now, weighed down with her riding clothes, she struggled helplessly. The edge of the nearest outcrop of rocks was within her reach, but it was steep and as smooth as glass, and her fingers clawed at it helplessly. To add to her difficulties, the water was icy cold, and something seemed to be dragging her down into its depths. Stories flashed through her mind – things she had heard about the tarn; that it was haunted; that it was bottomless; something about an old pit shaft. She kicked vainly in an attempt to feel the bottom, but her feet touched nothing. She panicked, raised her arms above her head and clawed the air, and as she did so she shouted, 'Help! Help! Oh, Jon – where are you?' Water

45

rushed into her mouth, closed over her head, and she sank . . .

The next moment she was lying on the bank, and Jon, wet and white-faced, was rubbing her legs and arms.

'Vicki! What happened? My goodness – I thought you were a gonner that time! Didn't you know this tarn is dangerous?'

'Well, I wasn't trying to *swim* in it,' retorted Vicki with chattering teeth, but something of her old spirit. 'Not with all my clothes on! I was trying to rescue a butterfly.'

'A butterfly?' Jon wasn't as astonished as some young men would have been. He could well imagine his own artist father risking *his* life for a butterfly.

'Yes – and that reminds me – I wonder what happened to it?'

They both stood up and looked down at the dark waters of the tarn – the sun had gone in again, and the wind had died away.

'There it is!' said Jon, pointing. The sudden rush of wind, combined with the splash made by Vicki's falling in, had caused a series of waves on the surface. The butterfly had floated across to the far side, and when they went round to investigate they found that it had crawled out by means of an overhanging clump of reeds and was now drying itself on a flat rock, opening and shutting its wings and quivering all over as its strength returned.

'If you only knew,' Vicki said to it severely, 'what a bother you caused, you'd feel ashamed of yourself, you careless creature!'

Jon, remembering the moment when he had come over the brow of the hill and heard Vicki's cry for help, and seen her struggling in the cold dark depths of the tarn, felt he could have put it stronger than that!

'Oh, Jon – you've got so wet rescuing me,' Vicki said, looking up. 'I'm so sorry! You were awfully brave to come in after me like that. Of course you know you saved my life?'

'Well, I can't say "no" to that,' laughed Jon. 'You certainly were in trouble, but anyone could – and would – have done what I did. As for being wet – I think we're both in need of dry clothes. We'd better ride over the hill to Todd's Rigg, the Dodds' place, and borrow some.'

Accordingly they saddled up Vicki's Maestro, and caught Jon's pony, Highwayman (Jon had flung himself off his back when he had heard Vicki's cry for help), and set off for the Dodds' farm.

'You know there are all sorts of stories told locally about that tarn,' Jon said as they rode away. 'They say it's bottomless, and that a "something" lives in its depths and catches hold of you and drags you down to its lair – a sort of water-horse, like they have in the West Highlands of Scotland.'

'Don't I know it!' shivered Vicki. 'I kept thinking of that when I was in there. I could positively *feel* it dragging me down!'

'Quite a few people have been drowned there,' Jon went on. 'And not so long ago some kids were camping here in the peel-house, and one of them – a boy called Peter somebody – was pulled out in the nick of time by one of the Charltons of Hordon.'

'What? You don't mean Uncle Guy!' exclaimed Vicki, nearly forgetting her dripping clothes in her excitement. 'Well, I must say it's just like him – he's always rescuing somebody. He saved my Aunt Jane from certain death on a mountain called Ben Cruachan in Scotland, you know. That was before they got married, of course,' she added.

Jon laughed. 'You make it sound as if he wouldn't have done it if they'd already *been* married!' he said. 'Well, here we are! It's a blessing the farm was just round the corner, so to speak. Let's tether the ponies to the fence and go round to the kitchen door.'

47

They beat a loud tattoo on the back door of the farmhouse with the butt of Jon's riding-crop, and although a dog barked incessantly from within, no one came to answer their knock. Suddenly Vicki gave an exclamation. 'Oh, how stupid of me! I ought to know better. Why, it's Tuesday, market day. The Dodds will all be at Hexham, and they certainly won't be back for hours yet – probably not till late tonight. Although of course *someone's* got to turn up before then for the milking.'

They looked at each other, while Jon shivered and Vicki's teeth chattered.

'What on earth shall we do?'

'Well, one thing is clear,' said Jon, 'we must find some dry clothes for you to wear even if we have to steal them!'

'And you, too, Jon,' amended Vicki.

'Well, I'll admit I could do with some dry things too,' he confessed. 'I wonder if they lock all their doors?' He tried the handle. The door opened, and they walked in. The barking dog rushed out, tail wagging, and promptly proceeded to lick Vicki's face all over.

'Fierce brute, I *don't* think!' laughed Jon.

'Oh, you old no-good-at-all!' said Vicki. 'Just supposing we happened to be burglars! What sort of a watch-dog do you suppose you are?' A few more licks were the dog's answer.

They went into the kitchen, while the dog jumped round them gleefully, giving little whines and yaps of delight. After all, he'd been alone since early morning, and he was a sociable dog. It had evidently been the Dodds' washing-day the day before, and the clothes rack was full of clean shirts and underwear of all sorts and sizes. Jon pulled down some of what were obviously Mrs Dodd's things for Vicki, and a vest and pants of some male member of the family for himself. They were all a great deal too big, but it wasn't the time to be choosy.

'Now all we need is something to put on top of this fine underwear, and we'll be all set up,' said Jon. 'Hey! Where are you going?' Vicki was leading the way upstairs. 'Golly, I feel awful – like a cat burglar!'

'You must stifle your conscience, old thing!' Vicki retorted. 'Look what I've found!' She had opened the door of a wardrobe containing what were obviously Mr Dodd's best clothes. Most of them looked as if they'd never been worn. 'Catch! One pair of riding-breeches of a most superior cut! One hacking-jacket!'

When the two of them came downstairs dressed in their borrowed clothing, they took one look at each other, and burst out laughing.

'Well, I must say we make quite good farmers – I should say a farmer and his wife,' laughed Vicki. 'Especially *you*, Jon! Those breeches fit quite well.'

'Sometimes,' said Jon seriously, 'I almost wish it were true.'

'What *do* you mean? You wouldn't want to be a farmer, would you? You'd have to work jolly hard! Personally, I don't think you'd make a very good one.'

'Who's to say I wouldn't? After all, my great-grand-parents (on my mother's side) were farmers, weren't they? Besides, that wasn't *all* the proposition.'

'Oh, you talk in riddles!' declared Vicki impatiently. 'Come on! I'm hungry, if you aren't. I'll just leave this note' (she was scribbling on the back of an envelope she had found on the hall-table) 'to explain things. Otherwise they might wonder where their undies and things had gone to. I shouldn't like Rover (if that's his name) to get the blame for having eaten them! . . . There! I'll prop it against the clock. Come on, Jon, hurry up!'

'Wait a moment,' said Jon. 'I want to talk to you. How old are you, Vicki?'

She stared at him. What was he after now? She never knew what Jon was thinking.

'I'm fourteen. I'll be fifteen next month. Why?'

'And I was seventeen last February. I suppose we're very young.'

'Of course we're young,' said Vicki. 'I really don't know what you're driving at, Jon, or why you should suddenly want to talk to me – in the Dodds' kitchen of all places! – about being young.'

'I was wondering if you had ever had a boyfriend?' said Jon.

'No, I haven't, and I don't intend to,' snapped Vicki. 'And if, by any chance, you're meaning *you*, it's like the song says, "Oh, no Jon, no Jon, no Jon, No!" I really don't know what's the matter with you today – you're being very silly. The man I *will* like will be at *least* thirty, and he'll have an interesting face – not at all handsome but arresting, if you know what I mean.'

'I do,' said Jon. 'You mean someone like your father.'

'Yes, exactly,' agreed Vicki. 'How clever of you to think of it! He will be very worldly-wise, like Papa, know how to order meals at restaurants when he takes me out, and how much to tip the waiters. And he'll never, never make me look silly. Well, to be quite frank, he won't be a mere boy like you. He'll be a man of the world . . . '

'No!' exclaimed Jon, cutting her short. 'It will be *me*, whether you like it or not. *Why* do you think I put up with a silly little girl like you? I'll tell you – just because I know you'll grow up to be the sort of girl I like.'

'Really,' drawled Vicki. 'And what about *me*, if I may ask? Suppose you don't happen to be the sort of boy I want, don't I have a say in the matter?'

'No,' declared Jon. 'A man has all the say when it comes to asking a girl to marry him.'

'So you say! But *I* might refuse you,' said Vicki with deceptive sweetness. 'Have you ever thought of that?'

'You wouldn't dare!' cried Jon.

'Wouldn't I? You wait and see.' Vicki was really only joking, but Jon was in deadly earnest.

'I shall wait until you're – let me see, eighteen – then I shall want my answer.'

'Well, you needn't wait – you've got it right now,' said Vicki. 'At eighteen I shall have just left the Royal Ballet School, and I shall be in the Company. I shall be on the verge of my career. My answer is *no*.'

'What do you want a career for?' asked Jon.

Vicki did a triple *pirouette* on a smooth patch of the Dodds' flagged kitchen floor. 'My, my, how old-fashioned we are! All girls have careers now. Didn't you know?' (She wasn't aware of it, but a conversation very like this one had taken place between her mother and her father nearly twenty years ago.)

'We'll see,' said Jon ominously. He looked out of the window and saw that the sun was no longer high in the heavens. 'Well, I suppose we ought to be going. I'm hungry after my unexpected swim! Let's ride back to the peel, and have our lunch there. But remember what I said, because I meant it!'

They rode back along the moorland path, and had their picnic in the upper storey of the rugged old building. Part of its south wall had been cut away, and a large wooden door substituted for the former slit-like window, in order that the sacks of grain and bales of straw could be loaded into the peel-house directly from below without having to carry them up the outside staircase.

Jon and Vicki opened the window, and sat in the sunlight, looking down over the little village of Garside almost hidden in its fir woods far below.

'You can see all the local landmarks from here,' Vicki

51

observed, pouring coffee out of her thermos into a couple of plastic cups. 'Look – there are the turrets of Uncle Guy's place, Hordon Castle, and away to the left you can just see the end of that funny house called Thankless. It's got a moat round it – you can see it glinting, if you get the right spot. Some people called Fenwick live there. Then almost due south of us, I can see one of the pepper-box turrets of Bychester, where that horrible Sir Nigel Monkhouse lives. He got married not so long ago, you know, to a widow. He *almost* married poor dear Sylvia Swan, but fortunately she found him out in time. *Just* in time – she ran away a day or two before the wedding! *I* had a hand in that,' she added proudly.

'It sounds like you!' laughed Jon. 'Yes, I agree – you certainly get a good view from here. I can even see Mintlaw, and that's not so very far from Granny's. There's an interesting old tower there called Dancing Peel. It must be one of the oldest buildings in Northumberland, because it didn't begin life as a peel-tower.'

'Yes, I just found out the other day, quite by accident, that the people who live there are called Dancy, and they have a daughter who's a ballet dancer. Her name is Annette. Of course,' continued Vicki, 'I've often heard of Annette Dancy – she's quite good, as a matter of fact – but I never knew she lived at Dancing Peel . . . By the way, would you like some more coffee – there's a little left.' She poured the rest of the coffee into Jon's cup.

'Oh, now you haven't left any for yourself.'

'I've had enough,' she told him. Then she stretched her arms above her head in an unconsciously graceful gesture. 'Oh, isn't it peaceful up here? Not a sound except the larks and the curlews. You know, Jon, sometimes I think I hate London.' She folded up her sandwich paper very small and put it carefully away in her rucksack. 'Just imagine what it will be like at this hour – all the Tubes packed to the eyebrows; everyone madly dashing about; your feet aching with having to stand and being trampled upon, and your arms with having to strap-hang . . . '

'Well, why do you do it?' demanded Jon.

Vicki shrugged her shoulders expressively. 'You know very well why I *have* to do it,' she said. 'It's because of Mummy, principally. Her heart's set on my stepping into her shoes. If only I wasn't so *good* – technically, I mean – the thing would settle itself.'

'Perhaps it will, eventually,' said Jon, pulling out a bale of straw, and propping it behind his back. 'You know, these things make pretty comfortable seats! . . . What was I saying? Oh, yes – after all, you're not in the Company yet – only for this one ballet. By the time you're eighteen, things may have changed.'

'Eighteen?' echoed Vicki innocently. 'I seem to have heard that word before! Momentous things are going to happen when I'm eighteen – according to you, that is!' Then her mood changed, and she sighed. 'Seriously, though, I don't see how they can. You see, I adore my mother. I just couldn't bear to hurt her.'

Jon pulled a piece of straw out of the bale and nibbled it thoughtfully. 'You know, Vicki – you're really *nice*,' he told her. 'I think that's why I like you.'

Vicki got up (she wasn't going to let Jon become sentimental again). 'Well, I think we ought to be going,' she said. 'I suppose you're staying with Granny Mason tonight? . . . It's good-bye, then, for the time being. See you tomorrow at eleven o'clock rehearsal. No rest for the wicked!'

They set things to rights in the peel-house, shut the big window, and climbed single-file down the steep little stone staircase to the ground.

'It's been a lovely day – in spite of the wetting,' Vicki said. 'I'll send Perkins over to Todd's Rigg with Mrs

Dodd's clothes, and perhaps you'll see about the things you borrowed. The postman might take them for you – postmen are obliging people in these parts!'

'OK,' Jon answered, holding Vicki's pony for her to mount. 'I'll see to it. So long, then! See you tomorrow!'

Vicki swung herself into the saddle, and was away in a flash. At the edge of the moor, where it dipped steeply down to Garside, she reined in her pony, looked back and waved. Jon was sitting motionless on his mount looking after her.

Chapter 8

At Mary Martin's

The day after her visit to the Royal Ballet, Nona was sent for by Miss Barnes, the Principal of the orphanage.

'I've just been having a little talk with Dr Johnson,' she said, 'and he thinks that you ought to have some dancing lessons to strengthen your back and shoulders.' She didn't express her own feelings, which were that, in her opinion, dancing lessons were a luxury – not for orphaned children. But she didn't believe in arguing with the authorities. Dr Johnson had ordered dancing lessons and, as far as she was concerned, that was that!

And so, by a mere accident – as is so often the case – Nona started off on what was to become her life's work – though many things were to happen, and many obstacles, some of which appeared to be insurmountable, had to be overcome before she was to reach her goal. Every Saturday afternoon, she went along to the Mary Martin School of Dancing, and joined the Grade One ballet-class. It was composed of small children of six and seven, and she felt very much out of place – rather like a huge Gulliver among the tiny Lilliputians. However, very soon Mary Martin, who was a sensitive and far-sighted woman (as well as being a first-rate teacher) moved her on to a higher grade, where the pupils were older.

'After all,' she said to June Robinson, one of her assistants, 'it isn't as if she were taking up dancing as her career, or even as if she were going in for any of the grade exams. She's here to strengthen her back, and she'll do it better in a class where she doesn't feel self-conscious. Of course, they'll all stare at her at first – it's only natural – but they'll soon get used to her.'

Mary proved to be right – in that last particular at least. The other children soon ceased to look upon Nona Browning as an oddity, and quickly accepted her as one of themselves. For one thing, she was soon the best in the class. The other children had many interests. In the winter, they went to parties, or watched television at each other's houses, or went to the cinema. During the summer, they played tennis, or went swimming. Nona, on the other hand, had only her dancing to live for. Up in the attic room at the orphanage, she practised her exercises, with the help of a chair for a *barre*. Some nights (with the permission of Miss Martin, and the co-operation of Gladys Makepeace) she stole back to the dancing school, which was fortunately quite near, and practised in one of the small studios. It sometimes happened that there was a class in progress in the big studio, and Mary, coming upon the pathetic child working at her *adage* all by herself, would invite her to join in. Soon she was dancing with the Elementaries, and holding her own! Her shoulders and back had straightened like magic, and she had a wonderful idea of showmanship, and an indefinable sense of what Mary called 'style'.

Very soon poor Mary was in a quandary. 'You know,' she confided to June one evening after class, 'that child Nona Browning is perfectly fit now. She's as straight as any of the other children – straighter than most, in fact! I suppose we ought by rights to tell them – the orphanage people, I mean – that further lessons aren't necessary. After all, she's been dancing now for over two years.'

'Oh, Mary – you *couldn't* do that,' said June, horrified. 'Why, the kid just lives for it!'

'I know! And you're right – I couldn't do it,' answered Mary. 'I'm afraid I'm very weak. That child has inveigled herself into the Elementary class, as you see, and I haven't the strength of mind to turf her out. For one thing, she's so good, and so *keen* – it's a pleasure to teach her. Oh, dear! . . . '

'I know exactly what you're thinking,' said June. 'If only she had been like the other children, it would have been easy. I'd say she'd have got into the Royal Ballet School without a hitch, but for that one defect.'

'Yes,' agreed Mary. 'But of course it's quite hopeless. She couldn't even teach, as things are – no one would understand her.'

'Going back to the orphanage authorities,' said June, 'one lesson a week won't break them. It's not as if you're charging for the others, Mary, and it keeps the child happy, so let's leave things the way they are.'

'I think you're right,' said Mary.

So Nona's classes at the ballet school continued, and she improved so much that Mary soon had her in the front row of the Elementary class when they did their *adage*. And then one evening Nona appeared in the back row of the Intermediates, and, as Mary said to June Robinson some time afterwards, 'I just hadn't the heart to turn her out, and in any case she might just as well be working with them as with the Elementaries. Believe it or not, before a couple of weeks were over she could hold her own with any of them, though most of them, as you know, are older and bigger than she is, and have learned much longer.' She sighed. 'Oh, June, if *only* . . . ! Here I am, waiting and praying for a child like her, one who's willing to work and work, and give herself unstintingly to her job, and now when I've found her, she has to be someone who (through no fault of her own) is quite impossible. It does seem hard! Oh, well – I suppose there's nothing we can do about it.'

'It's time we stopped talking about Nona Browning if you ask me, and went down to class,' said June, strictly practical. 'The Advanced will be waiting.' As they descended the stairs, the piano started up, and when they got to the door of the big studio, they saw that one of the students, at least, was hard at work on the *barre*. Only one!

'Nona Browning!' said Mary in a whisper. 'Oh, no!'

They stood for a moment, silently watching the dancer stretching and bending in time with the music. Even in these mundane exercises, the beauty and purity of her 'line' showed. At last Mary pulled herself together, and walked over to the child.

'Nona!' she said sternly. 'Whatever are you doing here – in *this* class?'

The colour flooded to Nonà's pale cheeks.

'Oh, Miss Martin,' she said. 'I do hope you won't be angry with me. I know I oughtn't to be here, but it's those *garguillardes* – they do them in this class, and I thought if you would just let me practise them here with the students, I wouldn't be the slightest bit of trouble. I'll stay in the back row, and you'll never know I'm there. Please, *please*, dear Miss Martin. I dreamt about those *garguillardes* last night!'

Mary had to smile. Imagine any other one of her many students begging, with tears in her eyes, to be allowed to practise *garguillardes*, let alone dreaming about them!

'Oh, very well,' she said.

Before the month was over, Nona was not only practising her *garguillardes* with the Advanced students, but doing them even better than they did. She kept her promise and stayed in the back row, but as for being unnoticed, Mary felt it quite impossible *not* to watch her most of the time.

'I give up!' she said to June, after an especially strenuous class. 'The child can come to the whole blooming lot, as far as I'm concerned! I'm expecting her to turn up to work for the Solo Seal any minute!'

Part Two

Chapter 1

The Blow Falls

Time went on. Nona Browning, now fifteen years old, still lived at the orphanage at the corner of Elswick Road, though her time there was quickly drawing to an end. She was small for her age, and very slender. The other children, when they wanted to be rude, called her 'skinny Lizzie'! Tommy Bates, still her enemy though he dared not now torment her, had been apprenticed to Vickers-Armstrong, but (while digs were being found for him) he continued to live at the orphanage. Jude, who was a month or two older, had gone to live-in with a family at Denton, and was working with a firm of furniture-removers. Nona missed him a great deal, though he had never taken much notice of her, except to see that she wasn't bullied.

And now came a certain day in spring – a day that stood out in red (or black) letters in the orphanage calendar, as it does in every orphanage calendar – the day of the half-yearly Board Meeting. Every inch of every floor in the ugly red brick building had been scrubbed; the curtains had been taken down and washed; the windows had been cleaned so that you could really see out of them; the faded chintz covers in Miss Barnes's sitting-room had been washed as well. Down in the dining-room, where the Board would have its lunch along with all the orphanage children, there had been a general spring-clean. Even the pictures had been taken down, and their glasses polished, till they shone like mirrors.

The Board was given a table all to itself embellished by several vases of flowers, and covered with a sparkling white cloth. The cutlery had been newly cleaned, though what the Board ate was 'exactly what the children had', as the Principal proudly pointed out. As a matter of fact, the food at the orphanage was good, if plain, and the Board had eaten worse at many a hotel!

There were two Board Meetings, one in the morning to go into the finances of the Home, with praise or censure for what had been done during the past six months; the second in the afternoon of a more personal nature. It discussed the merits (or demerits) of the various children, especially those who were due to leave the Home shortly.

'There's Sibyl Jones from Mrs Lorton's "family"', said Miss Barnes. 'Such a nice girl! She's fifteen next month. She wants to go into a shop. We thought about the grocery store at the corner of Denton Street. They're advertising a trainee's job for a girl of her age. I could get her into a family somewhere near who would give her a room and board for twenty-five pounds a week. The wage is only a pound an hour, so she wouldn't have a great deal left for pocket-money and clothes, but it would do to begin with. As you know, we give each child a set of clothes to go out with – not new, of course, but tidy.'

'Why do they all want to go into shops?' demanded Major-General Hunter, the chairman. 'She'd do better if she became a mother's help.' (He spoke with feeling, since his wife had had no help in the house for years.) 'She'd get as much as that, and all "found".'

'It's not a bit of good telling the girls that,' said Miss

Barnes. 'They don't like housework. They say it's too boring. Goodness knows why, since it's the best possible training for marriage, and that's what they all want to do in the end – get married.'

'Oh, well – let's get on.' (General Hunter was an impatient man and, although on the Board of Directors of the orphanage, he hadn't really much interest in its inmates, but only in its administration.) 'The next on the list, Miss Barnes, if you please?'

'Tommy Bates. He's placed, I'm happy to say, except for his lodgings, and I'm on the track of someone who I think will take him in. Meanwhile we're keeping him here (he's sleeping in the old sick-bay). Then there's Jude Dockerty, also in Mrs Makepeace's "family"; he's the child the police picked up running round the streets, you remember? A most satisfactory boy! We got him into William Holmes & Company, the Furniture Removal people, and he's doing well. He's got a room with a family at Denton. The next on the list is Robert Herd from Miss Jenkins's "family"; he's fifteen too, and likes doing things with his hands, so we got him into Flashlite Electric Works down at Blaydon; they run a hostel for their work people, so there's no further worry about *him*. That's all so far – except for Nona Browning. She's fifteen, too, but she's so small for her age, we haven't tried to place her yet.'

'She's the little girl with the hare-lip?' said one of the women on the Board. 'Poor child! And what does she want to do?'

Gladys Makepeace looked down at the polished table. She knew only too well what Nona wanted to do, but it was an impossibility. Moreover, even if it *hadn't* been, she was quite sure the Board (and especially Major-General Hunter) would think dancing a frivolous career.

'I have no idea,' she said.

'What about some housework then?' said General Hunter triumphantly. 'I'll ask my wife to give her a job.'

'I suppose she could have a week at our holiday camp in the Lake District before she starts, could she?' said Gladys Makepeace, catching Miss Barnes's eye. 'Then she could perhaps come on to you after that, General Hunter. Where do you live, by the way? In Newcastle?'

'Good lord, no!' said that gentleman. 'We have a place at Milburne, in Northumberland. But as a matter of fact, we rent a house each summer at Keswick in the Lake District, and, if I'm not mistaken, that's where your holiday camp is. By jove; it seems as if it's meant to be, doesn't it, ha, ha!' He was feeling jovial at the thought of securing a young helper for his wife. It would make things a great deal more comfortable for himself. No more washing-up!

Gladys Makepeace wasn't at all sure she liked the idea. She didn't like the Chairman – never had liked him. He was the huntin', shootin', fishin' type, and insensitive at that. She wondered how the shy, gentle Nona would react to this kind of household. However, she had no better alternative to suggest, so she said nothing.

Ever since Jude had put an end to Tommy Bates' bullying activities in so dramatic a fashion, Tommy had held a grievance against Nona and her protector. Nobody was going to knock *him* down and get away with it! Jude had left the orphanage, and was out of his reach, but Nona remained. He bided his time, and then, as the board meeting broke up, the opportunity presented itself. Or rather, it was more accurate to say that Tommy created the opportunity. He sauntered in from work, a pair of Nona's ballet shoes that he had taken from her locker dangling conspicuously from one finger, just as Major-General Hunter came out of the dining-room.

'Nona Browning!' he yelled at the top of his voice. 'Nona

Browning! Has anyone seen Nona Browning?' Then he added to nobody in particular, 'Or isn't she back from her ballet class yet?' Then, as Nona came running: 'Oh, I thought you mightn't be back. Found your toe-dancing slippers in the drive.' He tossed them towards her, carefully missing General Hunter's nose by inches.

'In the drive?' Nona's eyes were wide. 'I can't imagine . . . I must have dropped them as I came in.'

'What is all this?' demanded General Hunter. 'Have you no manners, boy? You very nearly hit me with those things! And what are they, anyway? Ballet shoes? What on earth are such things doing here?' He looked round vaguely at the bare walls of the orphanage.

'Oh, this is a broad-minded institution, sir,' said Tommy with studied insolence (after all, he had nothing to lose – he was seeing the last of the place any day now). 'You wouldn't believe the things that go on here – proper Butlin's Holiday Camp! Ballet classes every evening! Nona Browning aims to be a toe-dancer, don't you Nona?'

Poor Nona said nothing. General Hunter, also, was rendered almost speechless by sheer amazement and anger. He was old-fashioned, and to him ballet was a mere frivolity, and ballet dancers (he lumped them in with show business in general) a bad lot.

'Do you mean – do you really mean to tell me that *you*,' he turned to Nona, 'are being allowed – I may say encouraged – to waste your time learning to kick your legs in a dancing class? Why didn't I know about this before? Who is the person responsible? Who? Tell me, boy?'

'Well, Mrs Makepeace is her "mother",' said Tommy gleefully. He'd never liked Gladys Makepeace (she'd shown all too clearly that she didn't like *him*) so now he was glad to get her into trouble.

'Mrs Makepeace!' roared the General. 'I shall have something to say to Mrs Makepeace about this.' He turned to go up the stairs towards the corridor that led to the Makepeace 'family's' quarters, but Nona clutched his arm.

'Oh, sir,' she pleaded, 'please don't blame Mrs Makepeace. She's been so kind to me. And my ballet classes haven't cost anything – only the one Dr Johnson said I was to have for my back.'

'And what about the others?' demanded General Hunter, shaking off her arm. 'This boy said you were dancing every night. I suppose *somebody* paid for them?'

'No, sir – Miss Martin was so kind; she let me join in for nothing.'

'Well, I don't know who this kind lady is,' said the General sarcastically, 'but it seems to me that a lot of people around here are dispensing a great deal of mistaken generosity. How can you – *you*, of all children –' (he looked down at Nona, feeling only distaste for her affliction; no pity for her entered his heart). 'How can *you* have anything whatever to do with the stage, where all that matters is a pretty face?'

Nona was too polite to contradict him. She stood there, numbly waiting for the blow to fall.

'One thing emerges clearly,' went on the General. 'These goings-on must be stopped, and stopped immediately. This is a place for *work*, not frivolity. Mrs Makepeace must be severely reprimanded.' (Not for nothing was he an Army man!) 'As for *you*' his eyes gleamed with triumph as he stared down at Nona, 'you will be put into domestic service at the end of the summer. My wife is badly in need of some help at home, as I told the Board just now. It will be good for you to have something *useful* to do for a change. Well?' (as Nona said nothing). 'Can't you speak, girl? Have you no gratitude?'

'Yes, sir,' whispered Nona. Her world had fallen round her. The one thing in life that she loved was going to be rudely and cruelly snatched away from her. Up to this moment, she had scarcely thought about her future. In a vague sort of way she had imagined some sort of job (in a shop, perhaps) that would leave her free in the evenings to continue her dancing. But it seemed this was not to be.

That night the whole orphanage knew that Mrs Make-peace had received a terrible dressing-down from Major-General Hunter; that she had defended Nona Browning, and that the General had given her the sack. The children whispered among themselves, covertly rejoicing in Nona's downfall. That would learn her! That would teach her to give herself airs!

Nona crept up to the attic, and sat huddled in the dor-mer-window. Below her lay Tyneside, its teeming streets full of shouting, playing children, but she didn't hear them. She was numb with misery. The room grew dark, and Tyneside was now a glittering kaleidoscope of coloured lights. Downstairs in the orphanage, she could hear the inmates preparing for bed. They were flocking out of the dining-room (she could hear the scraping and squeaking of the chairs on the polished linoleum) and filing into the cold, square hall for Prayers. The sound of the wheezy American organ floated up to her; then the sweet, thin sound of the children singing their good-night hymn;

> *Now the day is over,*
> *Night is drawing nigh,*
> *Shadows of the evening*
> *Steal across the sky.*

The shadows had stolen across her sky right enough! She knelt down by the window and prayed: 'Oh, God – please, *please* make something happen so that I can go on with my dancing! And please – if it wouldn't be too difficult – could you make me less ugly. Please, dear God!' She imagined God as a benevolent (and sometimes stern) old gentleman living up in the sky somewhere, and bending down out of the clouds at intervals to listen patiently to all the requests sent up to him by His children. He couldn't possibly hear them *all*, she thought, but perhaps He would do something for her.

God does not always answer our prayers, however. Sometimes He knows that what we ask is not good for us; sometimes He leaves us to work out our own dreams, and again He sometimes sends someone else to lend us a hand. It was so in Nona's case, although it was to be quite some time before it happened.

Chapter 2

Preparations

As we have said, Mary Martin occupied a small flat above her dancing school, and every spring, about now, she and her second-in-command, June Robinson, would meet over coffee and sandwiches to talk over the details of the forthcoming Summer Show. This event was held each year in the Theatre Royal, and the proceeds were for charity. This time they were for the Spastic Children's Fund.

'It's queer how these things come round,' said Mary, pulling forward an easy-chair for June. 'Sit down, June, dear. It seems only yesterday that we were planning the last one! Well, thank goodness this year there's no problem about poor little Nona Browning, for she won't be here. They're sending her to that Holiday Camp of theirs at Keswick the week before the Show, and after that, she's going to work for the Chairman of the Board of Trustees, (though I don't think she knows it yet). Poor child!' She sighed – Mary Martin hated to see talent wasted.

'The trouble with you, Mary, is that you take everything to do with your precious dancing a great deal too seriously,' declared June, stirring her coffee thoughtfully. 'Anyone would think these children were your own children!'

'Sometimes I really feel they *are*,' confessed Mary. 'I must say, I grieve over little Nona Browning as much as if she was my own child. Well, to turn to more cheerful things – you'll be thrilled to hear, I know, that I've managed to get our dear Veronica to be our Guest of Honour, and to open the Show! Yes, and more than that – I hope that her little daughter, Vicki (actually she must be sixteen or seventeen now, but I simply can't believe it. For one thing, she *looks* such a child!), well, I quite think that Vicki will be coming, too, to dance as guest artist. I thought *Giselle*, Act Two. It would be a tremendous "draw", don't you think – Veronica Weston *and* Daughter! We ought to make oodles of money for charity.'

And so, sitting cosily over their coffee, Mary and June drew up the programme for the Show that (although of course they didn't know it) was going to change Nona's whole life. There was to be the usual number for the tinies, in which they lay on their backs on the floor (or rather stage) and did their limbering-up exercises. This always brought the house down! Then there was *A Tale of a Jack in the Box* for the Grade Twos. The Grade Threes were doing their 'set' RAD exam dance, which Mary had incorporated in a little ballet which she had called *The Examination*, and very charming it was! After this, there were two dances for the Evening Classes – one a Musical Comedy number, and the other, a 'tap' sequence from the Fred Astaire and Ginger Rogers film *Top Hat*.

After the Interval, during which the world famous *ballerina* Veronica Weston, would say a few words on 'Ballet and its place in the School Curriculum', there would be more dances for the smaller children, which, as usual would prove to be the most popular items of all.

'Do you remember last year,' said June, helping herself to yet another sandwich, 'when we had that awful little Cecil Davenport as the Wolf in *Red Riding Hood*, and that tiny Jennifer Smith *would* persist in playing with his tail?'

'Do I not!' laughed Mary. 'And suddenly he decided he couldn't and wouldn't stand it any longer – and really one could hardly blame him! – and he poked his head out from under the Wolf's mask, and yelled at her: "Give over, Jennifer Smith, or I won't 'alf give you summat"!'

'This year I think we'll play safe, and have Cecil for a Huntsman in *Robin Hood* for the Intermediates. Those girls are of a sensible age, and will keep him in order! Then after that, another musical comedy number. I thought of making up some dances to Strauss' waltzes – the costumes would be lovely – sugar-pink, blue and green, against a black back-cloth, and the male dancers in white silk tights, frilled shirts of the same colours as the girls' dresses, and black cut-away coats. It would be very effective!'

'And that only leaves the *pièce de résistance*, the real bit of ballet at the end for those at Advanced level,' said June. 'Act Two, *Giselle*, I think you said, with Vicki Scott in the principal rôle, and Hilda Steinberg as Myrtha, Queen of the Wilis. That's the part where the wilis dance round Giselle's grave, isn't it? Well, they've all got *Sylphides* dresses that would do, with a few garlands of leaves sewn on the skirts, and they could wear circles of leaves and white flowers on their heads – on top of their veils. It would be easier when they throw their veils away – they'd have something to get hold of, and also it gives them a bit of weight. Remember that time (I think it was the year before last) when we had bits of net floating all round the stage like a paper-chase!'

Mary laughed. 'Yes, I remember that. It's amusing to think of it now, but it didn't seem funny at the time! . . . I shall have to get in touch with Vicki Scott and find out her measurements. We must have a dress specially made for her that will match the rest of them. And she'll have to come to at least one rehearsal, because, although she'll certainly have learnt the rôle in the Theatre Class at the Royal Ballet School, she won't be used to dancing it with these students. I think we ought to make it the dress rehearsal, because that will be in the actual theatre.'

Chapter 3

Vicki Receives Two Letters

In a corner of the Senior Students' dressing-room at 45, Colet Gardens (the Royal Ballet School), Vicki Scott was reading two letters, or perhaps it would be more accurate to say she had just finished reading them.

'You look pensive, Vicki,' said Ann Johnson, one of Vicki's few friends (she was too acidly witty to have many!).

'So would you,' retorted Vicki, 'if you had received two letters each arranging something different for you to do in your one and only vacation, and both at the same time – well, almost! The first is from Mary Martin (you remember, I trained up in Northumberland at her school before I came here, and so incidentally did Mummy). Well, it seems she – Mary Martin, I mean – has persuaded Mummy to "open" her annual Summer Show. Also it seems that Mummy, knowing that I shall be on holiday at Bracken at the same time, has promised Mary that I'll dance the main rôle of *Giselle*, Act Two, as guest artist in the same show.'

'Well, what's wrong with that? You know it, don't you?'

'Yes, of course I know it,' said Vicki, 'but think how awful for me, Ann, to go to a blessed dancing show (yes, and the dress rehearsal, as well, so Mary says in her letter) when I might be riding, or – or doing other things.'

Ann stared at her curiously. There didn't seem to be much hardship to her in dancing as guest artist at one's own school. Think of all the applause one would get; the bouquets; the compliments! One would be a real *prima ballerina assoluta* for the occasion! Quite an attractive proposition, thought Ann enviously, and yet here was Vicki looking like a wet weekend!

'It doesn't seem to me to be too bad,' she declared.

'No, but wait – you haven't heard everything,' Vicki told her. 'I have another letter here, and it's from my Aunt Jane. She's not my aunt really, you know, but I call her that. She used to be a dancer too, but she gave it up when she married my Uncle Guy. He's not my real uncle, either. It's very complicated.'

'You've said it!' drawled Ann. 'Suppose you tell me about it.'

'I'll read you the letter,' said Vicki. She swung herself on to the centre table and sat there, cross-legged . . .

Hordon Castle,
Northumberland.

(Oh, yes, Aunt Jane lives in a castle, but of course it's a very small one – more like a fortified manor-house. Castles are two-a-penny in Northumberland!)

My dearest Vicki,

I am in rather a quandary! As you know, I never refuse to give my services in the cause of animals, or children. Well, we are having our usual Evening of Ballet in aid of the RSPCA here at Hordon on Friday, the 24th of August. It's all arranged, and several members of Festival Ballet are coming to dance for us – entirely free of charge, and all for the good of the cause. It's most generous of them! So far, so good! Now comes the awful complication. Last summer, I was staying at Keswick in the Lake District with the Craymores (you remember Stella and Jonathan?) Now I come to think of it, isn't young Jon doing something in connection with the Royal Ballet? Well, a group of young people in Keswick is getting up a series of entertainments to make money for a new wing which is being added to the little cottage hospital, and I very rashly promised to dance

71

in a ballet of their choosing (or, if I couldn't dance myself, to provide someone else). Now comes the interesting part – and the complication. They've chosen a ballet by Rossini (Toni Rossini, the choreographer, you know) called Planetarium, *and I'm supposed to dance the rôle of the Moon. Actually, I'd have adored to do it, as it's a wonderful rôle, but the trouble is they've chosen the exact date as our Evening of Ballet at Hordon – Friday, the 24th of August. The date can't be changed, either, because they're performing the ballet in the Druids' Stone Circle, above Keswick, which I must say will be the most breathtaking setting for it, especially as it will be full moon. This last point is why the date cannot be changed.*

To come to the point, could you, dearest Vicki, take my place and dance this rôle? I wouldn't ask it, but I do happen to know that you'll be on holiday at Bracken just then, so perhaps a day or two in the Lake District mightn't come amiss. The Craymores would let you stay at their house for as long as you wish. They themselves will be abroad, but there's a married couple – a Mr and Mrs Hewett – who act as housekeeper and gardener, and Jon Craymore may be there too.

'I haven't much doubt about that!' said Vicki, looking up from the letter, 'especially if he knows *I'm* going to be there!'

'*Why* don't you like poor Jon Craymore?' asked Ann. 'He seems so nice to me.'

'Oh, I don't actually dislike him,' said Vicki airily. 'He amuses me, when he doesn't get sentimental . . . Well, now you see how it is? I'll spend most of my precious holiday dashing about from Northumberland to Keswick and back again! The Keswick thing on the Friday, and Mary's show on the following Thursday. No, the Wednesday, because I have to be there for the dress rehearsal. I'll have no time at all to – to do what I want to do.'

'What *do* you want to do?' asked Ann curiously.

Vicki laughed.

'Oh, it's just an idea of mine,' she said enigmatically. 'I expect nothing will come of it. Anyway, I shall have to do what my Aunt Jane asks – she's such a darling, I couldn't let her down. It will mean staying at Keswick and rehearsing during the week ready for the ballet on the Friday, and then dashing back to Northumberland for the other. Fortunately I've danced the rôle many times in the Theatre Class, so as long as I turn up at the dress rehearsal all will be well!'

Chapter 4

The Camp by the Lake

It's strange how people's lives move, each in its own small circle, until suddenly one of them moves into the orbit of another circle. This is what happened to Nona and Vicki Scott. Once (on the stage of the Theatre Royal, Newcastle) they had moved very close to each other; had almost collided, in fact. Now they were moving together again. While Vicki was packing her suitcase for her stay at the Craymores' house on the eastern shores of Derwentwater, Nona was packing her kit-bag for her week at the holiday camp on the western side of that same lake.

Although Nona's world had fallen round her ears when her dancing lessons had been stopped and her much loved housemother had been summarily dismissed, yet she couldn't help but look forward to her holiday. For one thing, she regarded Keswick as her home, having lived there for so many years when she was a child. She was longing to see the mountains and the lake again. She couldn't, of course, remember the little cottage in the Newlands valley where she had lived as a baby but the holiday camp was only a short walk away, so she resolved to go there and see her old home.

When the bus reached the top of the hill just outside Keswick, and the children saw the little town lying below them, with Skiddaw, half hidden by cloud, towering over it, and the lake glinting in the afternoon sun, they gave a cheer. Nona's eyes were for Cat Bells. Just a baby mountain, it was, but it looked quite impressive from over here

74

with its shapely top, and the furry belt of woodland on its flank.

The bus inched its way through the crowds of tourists milling around Keswick's narrow streets, and in the market-square, for it was Saturday, and market day. The stalls with their fruit and flowers made a bright splash of colour against the grey stone houses and shops. The quaint Moot Hall in the middle of the square gave the little lakeland town a German look.

They left Keswick behind, and, having crossed the River Greta just beyond the town, they found themselves held up by the traffic lights at the second bridge across the River Derwent. They turned down the road to Buttermere just beyond the Derwent Hotel at Portinscale, and in a few minutes were driving slowly through beautiful wooded country, with Cat Bells rising ever more sharply in front of them, and Causey Pike to the right.

'Nearly at your journey's end, now,' said the bus driver, and he stopped at a gate barring the entrance to a private road where a wooden board said: 'ELSWICK TRUST HOLIDAY CAMP.' Again the children cheered. Many of them had been here before, so they knew it well. Through gaps in the trees the lake glittered invitingly; the bracken on the steep slopes of Cat Bells was just beginning to turn colour; the air was warm and soft, and the children felt in their satchels for their swimming suits. Only a few minutes now, and they would be in the water!

The Elswick Trust had bought a big old house standing by the edge of the lake, together with a crop of outbuildings, and had made the whole into a delightful holiday camp. They had felled the trees that shut it in, and now it stood in a semi-circular clearing, with the lake in front, and the misty blue hills of Borrowdale to the south. To the east rose Skiddaw, and its 'cub' Lattrigg. The outbuildings had been made into dormitories, and Nona and five other children slept in a converted stable, which still had a horse-shoe nailed to the door for luck. A loft, which was reached by a ladder, had been made into a bedroom, and in the mornings the children lay in bed looking out over the lake. As Nona said, it was like being in a ship at sea! How she knew this was questionable, since she had never been in a ship, but there is no doubt at all that it *was* rather like being at sea – especially as you could hear the water lapping against the disused landing-stage, and hear the seagulls crying.

At night, the only sound was the hoot of the owls in the Lingholm woods, but during the daytime it wasn't quite so peaceful. Groups of hikers walking along the lake shore would stop and stare curiously at the holiday camp. Often they would lean up against the railings, talking and laugh-ing, and sometimes they would watch the children swim-ming. Boats, weighed down with noisy holidaymakers, would stagger past, to be almost swamped by the wake of the launch as it deposited yet more holidaymakers on the shore. No, it was far from quiet in the daytime! Not that it worried the children; they were used to the noise and bustle of Newcastle. In any case, they were away from the camp most of the day. They were given free passes on the launches, so every morning or afternoon saw a party of them setting off for the Keswick Landings, or for one of the other jetties round the lake shore.

Nona and several of the other children climbed Cat Bells the day after their arrival, and had a picnic on the top. After they had finished, Nona went round and picked up all the sandwich papers and banana skins the others had dropped, and put them in her mackintosh pocket.

'Whatever are you doing that for, Nona Browning?' demanded Susie Baker, one of Nona's room-mates. 'We've finished with them.'

'It says on the dining-room door KEEP BRITAIN TIDY,' said Nona. 'So I'm doing it!'

'Don't be daft!' scoffed Susie.

'I think it's quite right,' said Nona. 'If we all leave our banana skins and papers and things on the top of every mountain we climb, they'll soon be nothing but rubbish-dumps!'

'Says you!' laughed the other children. Her words sank in, however, and the next time they went out picnicking, they took their rubbish home with them, and put it in the kitchen stove.

One wet day – the Tuesday after their arrival – Nona and five other children took the launch across the lake, and left it at the Barrow Landing. They walked up the Watendlath Road as far as the beautiful little pack-horse bridge over the Barrow Beck, and then found the footpath that leads over the top of Falcon Crag, crossing Cat Gill, and finally coming out on the top of Walla Crag. They had crossed the gill, when they saw the house.

'Oh, look!' cried Nona, and indeed the building was a strange one. It was made of grey-green Borrowdale slate, which made it melt into its surroundings in such a way that it was almost invisible until you came right upon it. In front of the windows stretched a mossy grass terrace, with cypress trees, cut into formal shapes, planted in it at intervals. Below, stretched other grass terraces – three or four of them – with stone steps leading from one to the other. Here and there under the cypress trees, or standing on the stonework, were white marble figures, some of them of undoubted beauty, but most of them minus heads, legs or arms.

'Ugh! It gives me the creeps!' said Susie Baker. She had to shout, because a waterfall, swollen by the rain, thundered down the gorge almost outside the front door of the house, and quite near where they stood.

'I wonder if anyone lives there?' said Marion Thomson. '*I* wouldn't if it were me. I think it's haunted!'

Nona shivered. The place was beautiful in a wild, desolate way, but there was a sad, melancholy feel about it, as if its owners had gone on a long journey, and the house, once loved and cared for, had been forgotten.

'I feel as if someone were walking over my grave!' she said.

They hurried past a little wicket gate, giving access to a weedy path that obviously led by a devious route to the back of the house, and hurried on to the top of Walla Crag, where the cold, rainy air and open views of Derwentwater and its surrounding mountains made them forget the strange sad house with its statues and cypress trees. As they walked down the path beside the Brockle Beck towards Springs Road, they came face to face with a large poster stuck on the end of a barn belonging to Springs Farm. Nona's eye caught the word BALLET, and she stopped to read it while the others walked on.

BALLET AT KESWICK!

A full-length ballet, Planetarium, *will be performed in the* DRUIDS' STONE CIRCLE, *on the night of the* FULL MOON, *Friday, August the 24th. Time* MIDNIGHT*! The dancers will be:*

Annette Dancy (Venus); Paddy Dolan (Sun); Marie Lavenche (Earth); Charles McMillan (Mars). By permission of Cosmopolitan Ballet.

Vicki Scott will dance the leading rôle of the MOON, *by special permission of the Royal Ballet School. A corps de ballet of children from the School of Dance and Mime, Keswick, will dance Stars, Moonbeams, etc.*

Note. *All these artists have given their services free! Please support them. Tickets £5 each. Proceeds to the Save the Children Fund.*

Nona stood so long studying the poster, that the others came back to see what was the matter, and now Susie was pulling her by the arm.

'Come on, Nona!' she said impatiently. 'Whatever are you reading all that stuff for? It's got nothing to do with us.'

'Oh, but it *has*!' cried Nona. 'It has to do with *me*, anyway. Can't you see it's all about a ballet they're doing tomorrow night in that place with the big stones, called the Druids' Circle. I wonder if Miss Proctor will let us go?'

'What – at five quid a ticket! What a hope!' scoffed Susie, who had by this time read the poster too.

Nona sighed. It was only too true. Five pounds was the amount each child was given at the beginning of the holiday for pocket-money, and it had to last a whole week. Most of the children (Nona included) had spent most of it already.

'Maybe they'd let us in cheap, because we're children.'

'Shouldn't think so,' said Marion. 'It doesn't say "children half-price". Besides, it's for charity, and that means they'll want to rake in as much money as possible. Who wants to go to it, anyway?'

'*I* do,' Nona said wistfully. 'I'd give anything to go.'

'Well, come on, do!' exclaimed Marion. 'I'm hungry, even if you aren't, and if we don't get a move on we'll miss the launch, and that'll mean no supper.' She dragged the reluctant Nona away from the poster, and the six of them walked down into Springs Road, and into the Castle Head wood by way of a short cut, which was a narrow lane running between two fields. In a very short time they had walked round the bottom of the wood, and were out on the Borrowdale Road. Then down another narrow lane, through Cockshot Wood, and out on the lake side.

'Quick!' shouted Dorothy Carter, the eldest of the six. 'There's the launch! It's just starting! *Run*!'

They ran towards it, down the rutty path, across the

79

road, down a flight of stone steps, and across the shingle. The man saw them, and waited till they raced down the gangplank, and tumbled into the boat, to collapse laughing on a seat.

'My goodness!' panted Marion, as the launch chugged away. 'There isn't another one for an hour. You nearly made us miss our supper that time, Nona, and all because of your stupid ballet poster!'

But Nona didn't hear her. She was thinking of the Druids' Circle, high above Keswick. How wonderful to see a ballet performed there! How she wished she could go!

Her wish was to be granted. Two tickets arrived with the compliments of the Committee for Miss Proctor the Matron and one of the older girls. Being well aware of Nona's passion for ballet, she decided to give her this special treat. Being on a Friday, it would make a good end to the holiday, for the day after, they would all go home, and Nona to her new job with Mrs Hunter.

Chapter 5

The Quarrel

Meanwhile Vicki had arrived in Keswick, and had attended several rehearsals of the new ballet *Planetarium*, in which she was dancing the rôle of the Moon. Her costume was a Greek tunic of yellow chiffon, and she had a glittering tiara of moonbeams on her head.

Contrary to what she had expected, she enjoyed staying at the Craymores' cheerful little Georgian house. It stood high above the lake, in a suntrap, sheltered from the cold east winds by Walla Crag, and from the north by the Castle Head wood. The scent of the flowers stole up to her bed-room in the mornings when she woke, and at night the rose-garden lay in a pool of moonlight. She would lean out of her window to feel the soft air on her face, while below her, beyond the garden, lay the lake like a glittering shield. Here and there among the dark woods on the opposite side, a light glimmered showing the whereabouts of a house. A small cluster of lights to the extreme right were those of the children's holiday camp, but of course Vicki did not know this.

As Vicki had prophesied, Jon had wangled a week's holiday, and had arrived at his parents' home the day after she did. When Vicki was not rehearsing, they went out together. One wet day they spent in Jon's father's studio – a huge attic that stretched right across the house, from front to back, and was reached by a steep little staircase.

'Oh, isn't it blissful to be able to work here all alone without being bothered by thoughts of dress-fittings, photographs, sittings and other horrors!' Vicki exclaimed, turning over a pile of canvases.

"'All alone!'" echoed Jon. 'I suppose you don't count *me*?'

'You?' said Vicki. 'Oh, no. As a matter of fact I'd forgotten you were there, Jon. I sort of take you for granted.'

Jon stared at her thoughtfully. Perhaps she was right, and she *did* take him a bit for granted. Maybe he ought to do something to show her he didn't intend to be taken for granted. Yes, that was it! But *what*? He couldn't think of anything.

'How long can you stay?' he asked, balancing on a pair of steps in an effort to look out of the sky-light. 'When do you have to go back to Bracken Hall? Not that it matters to *me*, but Mrs Hewett was asking. Meals, and so on.'

'I thought of staying on here until the Monday after the ballet,' answered Vicki. 'I might get a sketch of that quaint old mill on the Terrace Road, and one or two other things. Matter of fact, although I didn't want to come, I find now that I quite like it here.'

'If I was standing on *terra firma* I'd bow!' said Jon.

'You needn't bother,' retorted Vicki teasingly. 'I wasn't including *you* in my enjoyment.'

'Oh, weren't you? Well, if you want to go on staying here, you'd better *start* including me!'

'I was under the impression,' said Vicki, 'that this house belonged to your father and mother.'

'Usually the eldest son has – shall we say, a finger in the pie,' observed Jon. 'As I was saying, if you want to go on staying here, I shall require payment of sorts.'

'And what do you mean by that?' demanded Vicki. 'Because if you mean, can you kiss me, the answer is *no*!'

'I haven't the least desire to kiss you,' said Jon not altogether truthfully. 'What I meant was – I have a mind to paint you.'

'Paint *me*? I thought you only painted "flats".' (She meant of course, stage scenery.)

'I shan't make the obvious reply to *that* statement!' said Jon with a laugh. It was clear that Vicki hadn't the least idea that she had said anything funny. 'On this occasion I am shelving the scenery and painting the dancer instead. And by the way, I shall paint you in your Moon costume.' He had just seen Vicki wearing it for the first time at the dress rehearsal. 'I'll set you against a shadowy background of cypress trees, with a little bit of lake shining through. In that yellow dress, you ought to look quite startling.'

'Annigoni, in fact!' scoffed Vicki, though why she scoffed she didn't know, for she had a great admiration for the Italian painter. 'Sorry, Jon, but I'm not wearing that yellow dress, or *any* ballet costume for my portrait. If you want to paint me, it will have to be in my ordinary, everyday clothes – a jumper and skirt, or trousers or something.'

Jon broke into a hoot of laughter.

'My sweet, you're a ballet dancer, not a country girl! Whoever painted a dancer in a skirt and jumper!'

'Somebody's got to begin,' said Vicki lightly. 'You can set the fashion, Jon.'

'That I will not!' exploded Jon, becoming really cross. 'I want you in that yellow dress, or not at all.'

'I'm afraid it's not at all then,' said Vicki. '*I* didn't ask you to paint me, remember.'

'All right – then I shall go away,' threatened Jon. 'I've had about enough of this place anyway! Don't think I shall come back tomorrow either to applaud your stupid ballet either, for I won't.'

'I won't expect you to!' retorted Vicki.

And then Jon had left her, and she had heard him open the garage doors. A few minutes later his little sports car disappeared down the drive. Then he had really meant what he said, and gone. Vicki realized that she had carried her teasing too far this time. She had meant to give in about the yellow dress at the last moment (although she had spoken the truth when she had told him she didn't *want* to be painted in it, or indeed in any ballet costume). Oh, well – it was too late to repent now.

After Jon had gone, the little house seemed to have lost some of its charm for her. She missed him more than she thought she could miss anyone. For one thing, she now had nobody to tease and in the evening when she arrived at the tent which was to be her dressing-room – and which she shared with four members of the Ballet company – she missed him even more. All the performers, it seemed, had friends or relatives who were coming to see them dance. Only she, Vicki Scott, had no one who cared the least bit what she did, or how she did it.

'Mummy is coming all the way from Mintlaw in Northumberland to see me dance tomorrow night,' exclaimed Annette Dancy, who was Venus. 'And I expect Angus will be there too.' (She turned an excited *pirouette*.) 'He said he *might* manage it. Oh, how lovely everything is!'

What a vivacious little thing she was, thought Vicki enviously. And how wonderful to feel like that about one's dancing! And who was Angus? Her boyfriend probably. Well, *she* didn't feel wonderful about anything – she felt foul! And then, to make matters worse, Annette's mother had turned up at the rehearsal, and had looked in at the tent door. Annette had almost fallen over Vicki in her eagerness to get to her.

'Oh, Mummy! How lovely to see you! You simply can't imagine how much I've looked forward to it! Is Daddy here too? And Angus?'

'Not tonight,' said Mrs Dancy. 'But tomorrow they'll all be sitting in the very front row, and they'll have no eyes for anyone but *you*, Annette darling.'

'Oh, no – they mustn't on any account look only at me,' said Annette, taking her seriously. 'Why, there are lots of dancers here who are miles better than me. There's Vicki Scott for instance, from the Royal Ballet School. She's Veronica Weston's daughter, you know, and she's *wonderful*! I'd like you to meet her.' She introduced Vicki to her hateful mother, and Vicki had to admit that Mrs Dancy wasn't hateful at all, but charming. In fact all their mothers and fathers (most of whom seemed to have turned up for the final rehearsal) were charming. Only Vicki Scott had no one there – would have no one there at the performance tomorrow night to wish her luck at the beginning, or give her flowers at the end.

'My mother doesn't care the least bit what becomes of me – or Papa either,' she thought bitterly, as she changed back into her everyday clothes. 'Neither of them cares about anything but their own work – Mama her dancing, Papa his music. And come to think about it, Jon is just as bad! His art comes first, and everything and everybody else is just second-best.'

Chapter 6

The Druids' Circle

There were many anxious hearts in Keswick on the morning of the ballet. Would it be fine? Even more important, would it *stay* fine? Was it too bright to last? Vicki, leaning out of her window at seven o'clock in the morning, wondered if the bank of cloud resting on the tops of Glaramara and Scafell Pike would disperse, or if it would roll down the valley, as so often happened, blotting out the landscape in a pall of mist and rain. But by lunch time it was obvious that this was to be the day of days. The hills disappeared in a heat-haze, the lake shimmered, the Borrowdale Road lay baking in the sun, its surface oozing black beads of tar. The sun went down behind Cat Bells in a flurry of pink cloud, only to reappear again, like a temperamental *prima donna*, to make a final appearance in the gap formed by the Newlands pass and set a second time behind Grisedale Pike. The mountains floated in a sea of rosy clouds, and when the sun finally disappeared, the whole sky was suffused with a salmon pink flush. Dusk came quickly, as it always does in the mountains; the moon rose like a great orange Chinese lantern over Walla Crag, and beside it hung one huge, bright star.

At eleven o'clock the dancers began to assemble in the lane that runs down one side of the stretch of moorland where the circle of ancient stones stands. Here the tents which were to act as dressing-rooms had been erected, with a representative of the National Trust on guard to see that everything was in order.

By midnight the moon was high in the sky, and it was almost as light as day. The shadows cast by the great stones grew shorter as the moon climbed yet higher until it was directly overhead. Spotlights sprang up, manipulated by technicians hidden behind screens of branches; strange music played. The ballet was about to begin!

And now the dancers came from all sides. First, Venus and her attendants in glittering frosty white; then Mars with his followers in flaming red; then the Sun in orange, and Earth in nut-brown until the grassy space was full of whirling figures. The little stars and moonbeams in their glittering white dresses, danced on the outside, making a fringe of light.

Nona, sitting right at the front, sat still as if under a spell, as well she might. Surely never had a ballet been performed in so strange and unearthly a setting! And then, from behind a great stone not far from where she sat, came the Moon dressed all in gold, gliding over the dewy grass to dance a *solo* in the very centre of the Circle. Nona had often heard of, but had never seen, the world-famous dancer, Veronica Weston (though she had read everything there was to read about her) and here was Vicki, her daughter. Well, she was certainly a wonderful dancer, thought Nona, though there was a strange look on her face when the spotlight caught her in its beam, as if her thoughts were far away. In spite of the beauty of her line, and the grace and 'flow' of her movements, Nona felt sure that she wasn't happy.

Never will Keswick forget that night! The ancient Stone Circle with its surrounding mountains, Skiddaw, his crest hidden in light cloud; the dark ridges of Blencathra (the Devil's mountain) silhouetted sharply against the moonlit sky; Helvellyn, looking down upon the Vale of St John, shadowy, remote; the strange, unearthly music especially written for Rossini's choreography by Sebastian Scott. All these things created an atmosphere that took one back to the days of the Druids, when the Sun, the Moon, the Stars and the shadowy mountains were all part of a heathen festival.

'Papa's music reminds me a little of Stravinski's *Sacre du Printemps*' said Vicki to herself, 'though of course Papa's music is never *really* like anyone else's.' A thrill of pride shot through her, drowning the resentment she had been feeling towards her glamorous parents. Her delightful, brilliant, dramatic Papa! How she wished he could have been present tonight to hear his own composition in this wonderful place!

When the dancers had left the Circle and were back in their tent dressing-rooms, and the audience was streaming out of the main gate into the road to collect their cars, or to catch their buses, Vicki crept away by herself. Behind one of the great upright stones, she almost fell over someone else who had evidently had the same idea, and was standing on the far edge of the Circle, lost to everything but the beauty of St John in the Vale lying under a full moon.

'Oh, I'm so sorry! I didn't know there was anyone here! . . . '

'Don't go! It was my fault – I oughtn't to have . . . '

Nona and Vicki stood staring at each other for a moment, then Nona turned and fled. Here was the wonderful Vicki Scott herself! What must she think of poor Nona Browning with her twisted mouth?

As a matter of fact, Vicki thought: 'What a strange shy child! I wonder how she liked the ballet? What a pity she's gone – she would at least have been someone to talk to.'

Chapter 7

Rake House

The next day, which was Saturday, was one of feverish activity at the holiday camp. The children were being collected by special bus at noon, but before then, they had to give the camp a proper spring-clean, as it was the end of the season as far as the orphanage was concerned, and the camp was being taken over by a climbing-school.

When Nona and her room-mates had tidied their sleeping-quarters, they went down to the edge of the lake, and stood looking across the water to Keswick, still half hidden in morning mist. It seemed only yesterday that they had come and yet, at the same time, they seemed to have been here for ever. What a lot of things they had done in that one week, thought Nona! There were the excursions across the lake by launch; the picnic on the top of Cat Bells, and another on Causey Pike; there was their walk through Great Wood to the top of Walla Crag, and the strange house they had seen, with its cypresses and its marble statues; last but not least, in Nona's opinion, there was the ballet last night in the Druids' Circle. She felt she would never forget it as long as she lived.

Just at this moment, a whistle blew from the house to tell them it was time to go. The bus was to drop Nona at Rake House, where Major-General Hunter lived, and that was probably the last she would ever see of her fellow orphans, for they were all going to different jobs in the near future. She had got quite fond of some of them during this week's holiday, and would be sorry to say good-bye to them.

'I hope she's not a dragon,' said Susie as the bus stopped at the traffic lights over the bridge, beyond Portinscale. (She was referring of course to Mrs Hunter.) 'We all know *he's* an old so-and-so, but *she* might be better.'

Nona said nothing. Her mouth was dry, and a great wave of homesickness was engulfing her. The orphanage (and its once hated inmates) seemed like home to her, now that she faced the unknown. The bus was driving slowly through Keswick; it turned right at the Moot Hall, and swept through the narrow entry and out into the Borrowdale Road.

'Oh, I never thought of it being down here,' said Marion. 'Somehow I was sure it would be on the top of Manor Brow, or up there somewhere. I don't know why.'

They drove on past the church, leaving one or two big houses on the left, and now they were winding along the edge of the wooded Castle Head, the top of which, although they did not know it, was the core of an extinct volcano.

'Look, there's a house up there!' cried Susie pointing. 'That'll be it for sure, because there just aren't any more along this road.'

But the bus did not slow down or turn in at the gate, and they went on down the road. Nona, looking back at the little green house nestled on the southern slope of Castle Head, thought: 'Oh, how I *wish* it had been that house! I think I'd be happy living there – it looks so cheerful!' She did not know, of course, that it was the Craymores' house, nor that the girl she had met last night in the Druids' Circle – Vicki Scott herself – was at that moment eating her solitary lunch in the dining-room window, and feeling very sorry for herself. Vicki saw the bus pass, with the laughing faces of the children pressed against the windows, and thought: 'How lucky they are! *They* don't have to dance when they don't want to, just because their mother happens to be a famous *ballerina*! *They* have parents who love them.' She couldn't know that they were all orphans!

The road became narrower as the precipices of Walla Crag closed in upon it. The woods on its flank were at this spot dark and rank, the gloom only lightened here and there by the white spray of a splashing waterfall, leaping sheer down the mountain side. The lake was hidden from the road at this point, and there were woods on that side as well as on the left. Suddenly the bus stopped, and the driver looked round.

'Here you are,' he said, sliding open the door. 'Rake House. You can walk up that bit, eh?' He indicated the steep drive. 'Have to, anyway, cos it looks as if it ain't fit for a vehicle of any sort, least of all a bus! Seems they've got their garage down 'ere.' He pointed at a wooden building standing just inside the gates. 'Come on, out you get! We'll go on to the Lodore and turn round there.'

'Good-bye Nona,' said Miss Proctor. 'Be a good girl, and write and let us know how you get on. Remember all you've been taught, and don't forget to call Mrs Hunter "mam". You'll be well looked after by General Hunter, I'm sure.' She spoke more cheerfully than she felt. She was sorry for Nona. Such a little, white-faced scrap of a thing, and with that disfigurement to her face too! It didn't seem a very cheerful place to leave the child, but she had her orders.

'Good-bye! Good-bye!' cried all the children together.

'Oh, Nona – it's IT!' said Susie in a shocked voice. 'It's THE house, I mean. The one we saw that day!'

Nona got down from the bus, clutching her kit-bag in one hand and a rather tired bunch of wild flowers in the other. She had picked them that morning as an offering to her new employer. The bus driver got back into his seat, the door slid shut, and they were gone – her fellow orphans, all the family she had. She stood at the bottom of the drive and waited for the bus to return. Back it came in a few minutes, having turned round at the Lodore Hotel further down the Borrowdale Road. Susie and Marion were talking and laughing together, and the rest of them had seen a deer in the wood on the far side of the road, and were pointing it out to each other. None of them saw Nona. With a tightness at the back of her throat, she realized that they had already forgotten her!

She had, as we know, seen Rake House from the wooded path directly above it and had thought it a strange building, but now when she saw it from below, she thought it queerer still. The winding drive was stony and very wet, in spite of the fact that there had been no rain for several days. Between the stones grew fat cushions of emerald turf, and moss covered the trunks of the trees that closed in upon the path, until it was shrouded in a green twilight. The woods round the house were so dense that the lower branches of the fir trees were dead, and many had fallen off and were lying on the ground, half hidden by masses of ground-ivy, lichen, pine-needles, moss and ferns. The house, just coming into view above its grass terraces, seemed to peer down at her sadly, as if wondering what such a child should be doing in this spell-bound place. The waterfall she had seen from the path above descended through the dark woods in a series of cascades. In some places the drive crossed it by means of a stone bridge, or sometimes merely a large flat stone, and Nona, looking over the edge, beheld the water splashing down a green tunnel of ferns. The noise was deafening.

By this time she had come to the lowest of the grass terraces (she saw now that there were five in all), and it was a question of where she would find the back door. ('You must always go to the back door,' Miss Proctor had said.) Well, there was no mistaking the *front* door, thought Nona, looking at it in astonishment. There were pillars of grey

Borrowdale slate on either side of it, and the whole was enclosed by a tumbledown glass structure rather like a conservatory. There were several broken panes, through which the tendrils of a clematis had grown, and which looked to the frightened child like accusing fingers pointing at her. A short flight of mossy stone steps led up to this structure, and at the bottom, on a cracked pedestal, stood a marble cupid holding a broken bow. On the other side was a decapitated stone lion whose head glared at her from the undergrowth nearby. At the top of the steps, which merged into the rocky mountain side, was a headless figure holding a stone jar, out of which gushed water from a hidden spring above. Nona stared at all these things, her large dark eyes growing round with amazement and fear. The gloomy house terrified her.

A path winding up through a shrubbery of rhododendrons and azaleas led to what was obviously the back of the house. Nona followed this and presently came to the back door. A paved yard had been made by digging out the hillside, with the result that the back windows looked directly on to a stone wall, out of which sprang tufts of fern and an occasional primrose, only the yellowed leaves now showing. Nona stood for a moment quite still, while the splash of the waterfall beat upon her brain. Then, summoning up all her courage, she knocked timidly upon the door. At first no one came, and then there was the sound of high heels tap-tapping on a stone floor. The door opened, and Mrs Hunter appeared. She stared at Nona, thinking she was a hiker who had lost her way. Her husband had certainly not prepared her for this child, nor for the disfigurement that marred her face. She hadn't expected anyone so small, either.

'Well?' she said.

'Please, mam, I'm Nona Browning,' Nona said as clearly as she could. 'I've come, like you said I was to – I mean

Major-General Hunter said – and I've brought my things.'
(She indicated the kit-bag.)

'Oh—' Mrs Hunter stepped back into the stone-floored
lobby. 'I see. Well, you're *far* too small and young, of
course, but I suppose I shall have to take you for the week.
You do understand, don't you, that it's just for the week?'

Nona nodded. She didn't want to stay in this strange
house any more than its mistress wanted to keep her there.
She'd have gone that very moment, if she'd had anywhere
to go to.

'This is the kitchen,' said Mrs Hunter, opening the door.
'It's on the dark side, but you can have the light on. Electricity costs very little, as we get it from the waterfall. This
house doesn't belong to *us*, of course, as I expect you know,
but we rent it every summer – we have done so for years.
The quiet suits my husband.' (Evidently she didn't consider
the roar of the waterfall *noise*, thought Nona.) 'You'd better
take your things upstairs,' she went on. 'Your bedroom is
on the top floor.' She led the way up a narrow, twisting
back staircase, Nona following. Up and up they went – two
flights, three – their feet making a great clatter on the
uncarpeted oak treads. 'Well, here it is.'

Nona could have wept with disappointment. She'd been
hoping, as floor succeeded floor, that there'd be a wonderful
view when they got to the top. Now she saw that the little
attic room was a back one, and the window looked out into
the black heart of the wood. There was another small
window – a narrow slit-like aperture – at one side of the
room, and this looked out directly on to the waterfall, so
that it looked as if it was perpetually raining – and sounded
like it too!

'Have you got anything to wear?' asked Mrs Hunter,
obviously not very impressed by Nona's washed-out print
dress. 'I mean work clothes of any sort? Not that it matters
really, of course, as you're only here for the week.'

'Oh, but I've got a proper dress,' cried Nona. 'A dark blue one – nearly new – and an overall. And please' – she proffered the flowers which, by now, were looking very sorry for themselves – 'these are for you.'

'Oh – er – thank you,' said Mrs Hunter not very graciously. She took the nosegay with an inward shudder, wondering what on earth she was going to do with them. Half-dead wild flowers weren't in her line. 'They'll be nice for the kitchen,' she added.

'Oh, but I didn't bring them for myself – I brought them for *you*,' persisted Nona. She remembered the meadow where she had gathered them, the dew still wet upon their petals. Their loveliness had almost made her cry. It certainly never occurred to her that Mrs Hunter wouldn't like them. That lady said nothing more about the kitchen – she decided to get rid of the flowers later on.

'When you're ready,' she said, 'you can come down and wash up the lunch things.' It didn't occur to her to ask Nona if she had had any lunch herself. She went downstairs again by way of the front staircase, dumping the flowers in a handy waste-paper basket on the way. She'd pop them in the dust-bin later on when the girl wasn't looking. Not that it really mattered if her feelings *were* hurt, as she was only there for the week.

During the afternoon, she began to change her mind and revise her opinion of Nona. The girl had obviously been well trained by her housemother at the orphanage. She soon brought order to the untidy kitchen, washing the pile of dirty dishes (several days' accumulation), polishing the glasses and cutlery, and putting them away in the china cupboard. After this, she swept the floor, dusted the room and polished the linoleum. Mrs Hunter, who had been hovering in the background, began to look like a cat who has caught a mouse by mistake!

'I see you have been nicely taught,' she said grudgingly.

'If you've finished the kitchen, I'll show you how to prepare afternoon tea. My husband will be back shortly (he comes for weekends only, you know). I expect you saw our garage as you came up? It's just off the road.' As Nona didn't answer, she went on, 'My husband is always ready for a cup of tea when he comes in.'

'Oh, just like my mother!' cried Nona. (She meant, of course, Mrs Makepeace at the orphanage.) 'I used to give her one every afternoon when I came home from school.'

Mrs Hunter stared at her coldly. She didn't like chatty domestics. In her opinion, home helps (like children) should be seen and not heard. Besides, she found it very difficult to understand what Nona said. She went part of the way down the drive to meet her husband.

'Oh, George – the girl has come – the one from the orphanage, I mean. She's terribly small, and looks like nothing on earth, but she seems quite handy. We shall have to keep her severely in her place, though – she's obviously the sort that if "given an inch will take a mile." Answered me back quite pertly on one occasion.'

'Oh, she did, did she?' said General Hunter. He'd had his knife into Nona ever since the episode of the ballet classes, and now that he'd got her in his power, he was determined to make sure she behaved herself. He'd ram a little military discipline into her, or know the reason why! Ballet, pah!

'By the way,' he went on, 'I haven't put the car away. Old Johnson rang me up at the office, and it seems that he and Lilian are having a week at Windermere (son-in-law got a yacht, or something). They want us to go to dinner this evening – eightish. I said it would be OK.'

'Oh, George!' exclaimed Mrs Hunter in dismay. 'Tonight of all nights!'

'What's the matter with tonight? Had to be tonight, anyway. They go home tomorrow.'

'It's the girl,' said Mrs Hunter. 'Had you forgotten about her? She mightn't like being left on her first day.'

'Good Lord!' exclaimed General Hunter testily, 'if we are to allow our lives to be run by a twopenny ha'penny orphan brat, well, I ask you! Pity we got her! We'll be home soon after midnight, anyway, and she can lock the door and go to bed . . . Jolly lucky to have a bed to go to, ha, ha!'

The Hunters (Mrs at least) were not actively cruel people. They would have been horrified if anyone had accused them of torturing little Nona Browning. Why, they had opened their home to her, hadn't they? They had given her a bed and plenty of food. What more could they do? Yet Mrs Hunter felt vaguely uneasy when they walked off down the drive to pick up their car that evening. Nona's face, with its dark eyes and twisted mouth had an almost tragic look when she had been told of the arrangements.

'We won't be in to dinner,' said Mrs Hunter, 'but there's plenty of cold meat in the fridge for your supper. You can get what you want, and don't forget to shut the fridge door. You needn't wait up for us – just lock up and go to bed. My husband has a key.'

'You mean – you mean you'll be late in?' stammered Nona. 'You mean it'll be *dark*?'

'Now don't be silly, child!' exclaimed Mrs Hunter. 'What has darkness got to do with it? One is just as safe in the dark as in the light. Besides, God will take care of you. Darkness is very pleasant.' She really believed what she said – she was a woman of iron nerves, and it never worried her being left alone in the house – as indeed she was during most of the week. And as a matter of fact, Nona *was* as safe in wood-enshrouded Rake House as in a town house, with street lamps and a cinema round the corner. But you couldn't expect a child of Nona's upbringing to understand this, or to feel it either. Nona had always lived with other people – plenty of them. The problem had been how to get a moment or two's peace and quietness in which to think. The orphanage children had been taught that it is not safe to go out alone in the dark, and when they came home from school in the winter's dusk they all kept together. When they passed the mouth of a dark alleyway, they teased Nona, who they knew was timid. Once Tommy Bates had hidden at a certain dark corner of the stairs and jumped out at her. She had nearly died of fright. No wonder the thought of being left alone in the gathering darkness of Rake House nearly drove her mad with fear.

She watched the Hunters disappear round the first twist of the drive in a kind of frozen horror; then she ran like a wild thing into the dark rooms, switching on all the lights. One after another they sprang out of the dusk like brilliant glow worms, until the house was ablaze with light from cellar to rooftop – a glittering, fairytale castle set against its black overhanging crag. The Hunters would certainly have had the shock of their lives if they had looked back, but they didn't, and by the time they had reached the road, the house was hidden behind its encircling trees.

The next thing Nona did was to lock all the doors, but many of them had no keys, and the back door had only a rickety bolt that wouldn't have kept anybody out. She dragged a chair from the kitchen and wedged it under the door-knob . . . Now for the windows! She found that most of them wouldn't open anyway, but she managed to latch those that would. Then she fled up the back stairs to her little attic bedroom, slammed the door shut, locked it, and stood with her back against it, panting. Not for a king's ransom (or all the cold meat in the fridge) would she have ventured downstairs again. She'd rather – a hundred times rather – go hungry to bed!

Suddenly a dull, ominous sound shook the house. Thunder! The air was hot and still, and, through a gap in the tree tops, Nona could see the dark clouds boiling in the Jaws of Borrowdale, like some black brew in a witch's cauldron. Every now and then the top of a wooded crag, or a rocky pinnacle would appear out of the mist, and then disappear again like a phantom. It was like the ghosts of the mountains coming out and looking at her, thought Nona, terrified! The thunder of the Falls of Lodore added to that of the cascade that leapt from rock to rock outside her window, and the runnels of water splashing down from every crag and gully, was like the noise of an express train emerging from a tunnel. Evidently there had been a cloud-burst on the tops, and every little stream had become, in a matter of seconds, a foaming torrent.

There was another crash of thunder, which went echoing round the mountains; then a blinding zigzag of lightning which split the inky clouds, followed by a splintering crack. One of the trees in the drive had been struck, and smoke, smelling of sulphur, was rising from it. Panic seized Nona. She fled down through the house, wrenched open the back door, and made for what she thought was the path up through the wood leading to the little wicket gate they had seen that day when they had walked over Walla Crag. But where was the path? She couldn't find it. Water was streaming off the mountain side, and pouring in torrents off the black rocks. She staggered on. In her panic, she had mistaken the bed of the stream for the path. In the last few minutes, the waterfall had risen and she found herself struggling up a wide cascade. Stones hurtled down the steep hillside, missing her by some miracle, cold waves of water flung her, gasping, from rock to rock. She was covered with leaves, and bits of moss; smothered by flying spray. She gave a terrified scream; then another . . .

Chapter 8

Thunderstorm

Meanwhile Vicki watched the bus containing the orphan children disappear down the Borrowdale Road, and sighed. They all looked so happy, and she was so lonely! After she had finished her meal, she piled the dishes on to a tray, and carried it through into the kitchen, where she dumped it down on the draining-board. Mr and Mrs Hewett had gone off to Carlisle in their car, and wouldn't be back till late that night.

'I'll do the dishes tomorrow,' Mrs Hewett had said to Vicki before she went. 'Just you pile them in the sink, and run the cold water tap over them.'

Vicki, who was anything but domesticated, was only too glad to turn her back on them! She wandered round the house, up and downstairs, and finally settled down in the studio to finish a sketch she had begun the day before. She felt lonelier every minute, which was strange, she thought, because usually all she wanted was peace and quiet. Well, she had peace and quiet here, all right, and yet she wasn't happy. Oh, well – tomorrow she would go back to Bracken. She would have packed her bag and gone now, but the Hewetts might be offended, and besides she hadn't enough money for her railway ticket – she would have to borrow some from them when they returned. All Jon's fault, she thought furiously. He'd promised to take her home in his car, and so she had spent more money than she would have done on the lovely semi-precious stone jewellery one finds in the Keswick shops. Opening her handbag, she counted her money. She had only about three pounds left.

After tea, she went out into the garden and drew in her breath at the matchless view. It was as dramatic as a stage setting! Thunder clouds were gathering at the head of the valley, the rocks were the colour of ripe black grapes. A shaft of sunlight, slanting between two ink-black clouds, fell upon the lake, turning it to a sheet of steel. Walla Crag loomed so close in the damp air that she felt she could almost touch the trees on its slopes. She climbed the wall that surrounded the Craymores' land, and set off over the fields towards the Crag. She would walk along the woodland path from Rake Foot over the face of the Crag to where it dived down among the trees to join the Borrowdale Road a few miles further on. She might catch a bus home from there, if she was lucky. At all events, it would be something to do. She only hoped it wasn't going to thunder!

The path lay baking in the sun, and Vicki was glad when it entered Great Wood and she was in the welcome shade of the trees. Even in her short-sleeved, low-necked summer dress she was breathlessly hot. Not a leaf stirred, and the air seemed to press down upon her, charged with electricity. It made her head ache. The sky grew darker, until she could hardly see the path, although it was only six o'clock. There was an ominous rumble, telling her only too plainly that her fears about the thunderstorm were about to be realized. Rain spilled down through the branches and fell with delightful coolness upon her bare arms. In a few minutes, however, it was clear that unless she got shelter – and quickly! – she would be wet through. She stopped short in her tracks. Should she go on and somehow get down to the Borrowdale Road and a possible bus, or go back the way she had come? She decided on the former, for at least she would have the woods to shelter her.

She set off again at a run, jumping over branches and

roots in a desperate effort to beat the storm. The rain began to fall faster and faster, until it was a wall of shining steel slanting down through the trees. In a very short time she was wet through, her shoes balls of mud, and the rain was running off her hair in rivulets.

She paused for a moment to get her breath, leaning with her back against a tree. And then, while she stood there, she saw an amazing sight. Just below her, on a little rocky shelf jutting out from the mountain side, surrounded by trees, was a house. There was nothing very strange about that, of course – people build their houses in all sorts of strange places in the Lake District – but this house looked like an outsize chandelier hanging from the black rocky cliff. Lights blazed from every window, lighting up the most fantastic garden Vicki had ever seen. A collection of marble statues stood in various attitudes of abandonment. A waterfall, swollen by the thunder rain, rushed down past the house in a smother of white foam.

'My goodness!' exclaimed Vicki. 'I wonder who lives there? They must be having a party!' She decided to climb down to the house – it was too dark to see if there was a path – and ask for shelter. They could hardly refuse she thought, even if they *were* having a party. Perhaps if she were lucky they might offer a change of clothing. She set off down the mountain side, stumbling over stones, and tripping over roots, sometimes nearly falling headlong. And then a scream (only just heard above the roar of the water, and the swish of the rain in the treetops) reached her ears. Then another, and another.

'I'm coming!' she shouted instinctively, and plunged in the direction of the sound. The thunder rolled again; there was a vivid flash, and by its light Vicki saw a figure struggling on the edge of the waterfall. It floundered against the slippery rocks, and seemed in danger of being washed away at any minute. 'Here! This way!' Vicki shouted again. She made for the waterfall, and then, by the light of a second flash, she managed to grab a handful of clothing. A second later she had pulled the figure clear of the water. It stood upright, and she saw with amazement that it was the little girl she had met the night before at the ballet in the Druids' Circle. She was a pathetic sight, hair plastered down on each side of her white disfigured face, tragic dark eyes, cotton frock clinging to her legs in wet folds. They were both so surprised that they stood still for a moment just looking at each other. Vicki recovered first.

'Whatever were you doing walking up the waterfall?' she demanded.

'I d-didn't kn-know it w-was the – waterfall,' shivered Nona. 'It was dark, I couldn't see. I thought it was the s-stony p-path.'

'No doubt it *was* – before the thunderstorm,' admitted Vicki. 'Paths are apt to become waterfalls at any minute in this part of the world. By the way, do you live here?' She indicated the house.

'N-not really,' answered Nona. 'I'm supposed to be the m-maid. I've only just come. They went out to dinner and left me alone, and then the thunder came, and I was f-frightened. You see—' Out it all came. The orphanage and Tommy Bates. Jude, her deliverer; the children who mocked and tormented her because of her lip; the dancing classes to cure her drooping shoulder; Major-General Hunter—

'You mean, you can *dance*?' broke in Vicki, who had only understood half of what the child said, but had caught the word 'ballet', and 'Miss Martin', and had got the general idea. 'You say you trained with Mary Martin in Newcastle?'

Nona nodded eagerly.

'I simply can't believe it!' exclaimed Vicki. 'Why, *I* trained there myself – before I went to the Royal Ballet School. And you say you're the Hunters' maid? Why, I know them – at least, I've heard of them. My papa and General Hunter are sworn enemies! You said they'd gone out and left you, so I gather there's no one in the house?'

Again Nona nodded.

'Well, come on then!' said Vicki, seizing the child's arm. 'What are we waiting for? I'm wet, and you're wetter. I can borrow some of Mrs Hunter's clothes, and you'll have some of your own in there, I suppose.'

Clinging closely together, and making use of the dazzling flashes of lightning, they managed somehow to get back to the house. They let themselves into the kitchen; then stood looking at each other, while their clothes dripped on the flagged floor. Vicki began to laugh.

'I can just imagine what we look like!' she said. 'Well, let's rummage! I suppose you don't know which is Mrs Hunter's bedroom? No? Never mind – we'll find it.' She set off upstairs followed by Nona. They opened one door after another, and finally found the room. It was only too obviously Mrs Hunter's, since she had left her clothes lying on the chairs and the bed. Vicki picked out a skirt and jumper (much too large for her) and put them on, while Nona watched her nervously.

'Do you think we ought—?'

'It's all right,' Vicki assured her. 'I'll let her have them back safe and sound. After all, if she'd been here she'd have had to lend me something, and she oughtn't to have gone out and left you all alone. She must be a gorgon! . . . Now, what about you? Where's your room?' They went up to the attic, and Nona changed into dry clothes.

'And now I think we'd better go down and turn off all those lights,' said Vicki after they had finished. 'I know you meant it for the best – to cheer you up and so forth – but it *does* rather advertise the house, don't you think!

Goodness knows who might turn up to see what the blaze is about! The fire-brigade probably!'

They went downstairs, switching off the lights as they went, Vicki talking all the time and Nona listening, wide-eyed.

'You know, I've just tumbled to it – this must be Rake House. I've heard about it. Two people with lots of money built it when they married a very long time ago. All these statues and vases and things they brought from Pisa in Italy, where they went for their honeymoon. It must have been a lovely house then, because all these trees were small, and you would be able to see the lake, although of course the house wouldn't get much sun, even then, because of the crag above it. But as they only came in the spring and summer, it didn't matter. They spent their winters in Italy, and then one year the wife came back alone – her husband had died out there. She dismissed all the servants (they had plenty in those days!) and lived like a recluse, until eventually she died too (they said of a broken heart). Her nephew, who inherited the house, couldn't live in it because he had married a South African woman, and settled in Cape Town. Nobody would buy the house, because by then the trees had grown up, and it looked like the Sleeping Beauty's palace, and anyway, nobody wants to live in a house like this nowadays – especially in the winter; it costs too much to keep it warm. So the place has been let during the summer months only, and it's got dreadfully neglected . . . Mrs Hewett (she's housekeeper to the people where I'm staying) told me about it.'

They had got down to the drawing-room by this time, and Vicki looked round her curiously. It was a strange room, full of curious cabinets and inlaid tables. The large bay window was enclosed by the tumbledown conservatory Nona had seen from below when she had first arrived, and the long tendrils of creepers and vines growing over the glass and hanging through the broken panes, kept out what light there was (now that the thunderstorm was passing over, it was not quite so dark). Adding to the eerie effect was the tap-tap of a broken shutter banging gently against the wall outside.

'Well,' said Vicki after they had stood in the doorway for a few minutes in silence, 'it's not exactly a *cheerful* room, is it, but at least it's *big* and it's got a parquet floor. We can use it for a studio. Take off those awful slippers (Nona had, of course, left her wet, muddy shoes in the kitchen with Vicki's when they had come back to the house), and let's see you dance. What do you know? Ever done Odette's solo from *Swan Lake* – where Odette first sees the Prince?'

Nona nodded, and while Vicki hummed the music, she danced. At the end, she turned to the elder girl, dumbly awaiting the verdict from the daughter of the famous *ballerina*.

'You're good – frightfully good I'd say,' pronounced Vicki. 'Turn a *pirouette*.' Nona turned a triple. 'Now an *arabesque* – yes, *penchée* – *attitude* – can you execute an *entrechat*? Oh, good! A *six*! . . . Well, all I can say is that you're wasted as Mrs Hunter's maid – that is, unless of course you *want* to be a maid. Do you?'

Nona shook her head. 'No,' she said emphatically. 'But I expect it's what I've got to be, all the same.'

'Now look,' Vicki, spoilt only daughter of famous parents, couldn't understand Nona's resigned attitude at all, 'you must show a bit of spirit, or you'll never get what you want. To begin with, this place:' (she looked round the eerie room) 'you obviously can't stay here. If they behave like this to you on your first day, goodness knows what they'll be like at the end of a few months. You *must* get away. You must leave a note giving them notice, and come home with *me*.'

'Home with you?' echoed Nona.

'Well, it's not my home really. My real home is in North-umberland, of course, but I'm staying with the Cray-mores at their house not far from here. Oh, don't worry,' (as Nona looked startled) 'the Craymores aren't there – they're abroad. Well, how about it?' She looked at Nona enquir-ingly. 'You can't stay here all by yourself – you daren't. I can see that!'

'No, no!' cried Nona, when Vicki got up as if to go. 'I can't stay here alone – I'd die of fright! Please, *please*, Miss – Miss – don't leave me.'

'Vicki is my name,' said Vicki. 'There you are, you see – you *must* come with me. As a matter of fact, I have a vague sort of plan for you, but it means both of us getting back to Newcastle. No, don't ask me any more just now – I've got to work it out. Well, if you're decided, I think we ought to leave a note for them.' She rummaged in an antique desk that stood near the window, found a sheet of notepaper and a pencil, and scribbled a line or two.

Dear General and Mrs Hunter,

I find that I cannot be your maid after all, so please accept one day's wages in lieu of notice ('in lieu' means 'instead of', explained Vicki. 'It sounds more professional!') *I have gone back to Newcastle with a friend, because I daren't stay here all by myself. I shall be quite safe, so you need not worry about me.*

Yours sincerely –Vicki stopped writing, and looked up at Nona. 'What's your name, by the way? I mean your second name?'

'Browning,' said Nona.

Yours sincerely,

Nona Browning, wrote Vicki. 'By the way, what wage was the old bag giving you?

'Fifteen pounds a week,' answered Nona.

'It's far too little,' Vicki declared, going back into the kitchen, 'but it makes things easier. I haven't got that much with me, but I can leave something. She pulled her purse out of the pocket of her wet dress and counted out the last of her money for the second time that day. Nona watched her puzzled.

'But why? I haven't had *any* money from her yet—'

'No,' said Vicki, 'but you see it works both ways – this "giving notice" idea. If Mrs Hunter had dismissed *you* without notice, you'd have been in your rights to demand a *week's* wages, and so, as you're leaving *her* without notice, she's entitled to something – although I think that she's acted so badly that she doesn't deserve anything at all – and besides, I haven't got enough to pay her for the week. Still, this may help to "soothe the savage breast" when she comes back and finds that the bird has flown and she's lost her domestic help – especially at fifteen pounds a week! Well, now let's go back upstairs and pack up your things. You say the Hunters have gone to Windermere? In that case they can't get back for hours yet – still, you never know – they *might* get a puncture on the way and turn round and come back, or Mrs Hunter's conscience *might* smite her – anyway, it's best for you to flit while the flitting's good! That is, if you really want to throw in your lot with me.'

'Oh, I do, I do!' cried Nona. Vicki seemed to be the only friend she had in the world.

Chapter 9

The Idea

Never had Nona seen such a lovely house as the Cray-mores'! When they arrived, tired and footsore from their long walk along the Borrowdale Road, and turned in at the gate at the bottom of the drive leading up to the little house on the hill, she exclaimed in delight, 'Why, it's the house I saw from the bus! I was so hoping it belonged to the Hunters.'

'Not it!' said Vicki. 'It's far too nice for the likes of them! As I told you, it belongs to some friends of mine – or rather, my mother's, and I adore it! By the way, do you mind sleeping in Jon's room? I wouldn't ask you only the bed's all made up, and it'll save an awful lot of bother? Oh, Jon's the son of the house,' she added, seeing the question in Nona's eyes. 'He was staying here until yesterday, and then we quarrelled because I wouldn't let him paint me in a ballet dress, and he went off in a huff to stay with his grandmother (great-grandmother, actually) in Northumber-land. He's very fond of her – she's nearly a hundred . . . Oh, here he is!'

Nona turned in alarm, expecting to see a strange young man, but instead she found Vicki standing in front of a grand piano upon which stood a photograph of a dark, clever-looking boy, with a signature, Jonathan Richard Craymore, scrawled underneath.

'Oh, I think he's wonderful!' said Nona. 'I mean, I think he *looks* wonderful. Is he your boyfriend?'

Vicki blushed.

'No, of course not – what an idea!' she said a shade too emphatically.

'I'll bet he wants to be!' declared Nona.

'Thank you,' Vicki said mockingly. 'Jon and I get on rather well as a general rule, but at the moment I'm terribly annoyed with him. You see, he was supposed (I mean he *offered*) to take me home – back to Northumberland – in his car, and now I'm left flat broke. I shall have to borrow some money from the Hewetts, and I hate having to do that. To do him justice, though,' she continued, 'Jon didn't realize my financial situation.'

Nona listened to her, not realizing the meaning of half she said. It was almost as if she spoke in another language.

They went to the kitchen, and found that Mrs Hewett had left a dish of macaroni cheese in the fridge ready to be heated up, so Vicki put it in the oven, while Nona filled the kettle.

'I can't think what's happened to them – the Hewetts, I mean,' Vicki said, when the clock in the hall struck nine, and still there was no sign of the housekeeper and her husband. 'They said they'd be back soon after eight, and they're most reliable people. I suppose their car must have gone wrong.'

It was while they were having their meal that the telephone rang. Vicki sprang up from her chair. 'It'll be the Hewetts! Excuse me, please – I must go and answer it.' She came back a few minutes later with a grave face. 'That was a call from Carlisle Infirmary,' she said. 'The Hewetts have been hurt in a car crash. I thought it wasn't like them to be so late when they knew I was here alone. The poor things have been taken to hospital with concussion. Oh, they're not seriously injured,' she added, seeing Nona's frightened face. 'At least, the person I spoke to *thinks* they aren't, but they certainly won't be out of hospital for a day or two – probably not for about a week – and that makes it very awkward for *us*. Especially as I have no money. I left my cheque book in London and no one knows me here, so that's no use, and anyway I have a gloomy feeling that my account is overdrawn as it is. I suppose I *could* go in and plead with the bank manager, but tomorrow's Sunday, so that's no use either. Oh, dear! We're certainly in trouble!' She had been speaking half to herself all this time, and in any case all this talk of cheques and banks meant nothing at all to the little orphan girl who had never owned more than a few pounds of holiday money in her life.

'There's only one thing for it – we must hitch-hike,' declared Vicki. She turned to Nona 'Are you game?' Nona, who knew all about this form of transport, said at once. 'Oh, yes – let's!'

'I know it's all wrong really to do it,' went on Vicki. 'At least, Papa says so. He says if you can't afford to pay for where you want to go, you oughtn't to go there at all. He calls it cadging to beg lifts from other people. But there *are* occasions (one might really call them emergencies) when it's permissible. As a matter of fact, I remember Papa telling me how he and my mama begged a lift into Newcastle when they were stranded in the fog. They were about the same age as us, or a bit younger, and if they hadn't done it, my mama might never have become a *prima ballerina*. So we have a precedent.'

'A what?' asked Nona.

'Well, I mean we have their example before us,' explained Vicki. 'I know it's still a little different, because we're girls, but there are *two* of us, which makes it better. Anyhow, it's our only chance of getting to Newcastle in time for the dress rehearsal at Mary's . . . Oh, yes, I see I must explain a bit,' she added, seeing Nona's amazed expression. 'You may or may not know that I am dancing the rôle of Giselle at Mary's Show on Wednesday.'

'Oh, yes,' cried Nona. 'Miss Martin told us about it. She was ever so thrilled!'

'Well, *you*, my darling Nona, are going to take my place at the dress rehearsal, and dance instead of me. Now don't ask me to explain any more just now, because I still haven't got it all worked out, but the most important thing is for us to go *now*, and practise. You must be *perfect*, and you must dance as you've never danced before, because your whole life will depend upon that dress rehearsal!'

They went up into the big studio, and rolled back the carpets.

'What a good thing Jon has a tape-recorder here,' Vicki said. 'Anyway, I have *Giselle* with me to run through. Could anything be better? Do you know the rôle at all?'

Nona explained that she had watched several rehearsals of the coming show at Mary Martin's, and had even danced the rôle of Giselle once or twice with Peter Wright who was dancing Albrecht, when Greta Maynard, who was understudying Vicki, had been away. In a few minutes Vicki found that Nona really knew the rôle, and all that was needed was practice, and a final polishing up.

Again and again they went through the rôle – Vicki taking first the part of Myrtha, Queen of the Wilis, and then that of Albrecht, the Prince, who has betrayed Giselle and been the cause of her death. Sometimes she even took the part of Hilarion, the Gamekeeper. She found that Nona was full of intelligence, and not only that, but she had lived for her dancing, and for that alone, and so she was able to do what few students could have done – learn a difficult rôle overnight.

'Of course, you can't expect to be perfect,' said Vicki, when they stopped for a rest. 'It would take weeks and months to do that, and however long you dance Giselle, you're always learning more about the rôle. But at least you can dance the *solo*, and the *pas de deux* with Albrecht, beautifully. Now let's try that part again. It's only half-past eleven . . . you emerge from your grave and curtsy to me. I'm the Queen of the Wilis.'

'But when you – I mean the Queen of the Wilis – plucks off my veil, everyone will see that it's *me*, and not you,' objected Nona.

'No, they won't, my dear,' answered Vicki, 'because the Queen of the Wilis isn't going to pluck off your veil – she's going to forget!'

'Oh! But how—'

'Yes, I'm going to engineer it. After all, it's only the dress rehearsal, so it doesn't *really* matter what happens. Mary will be furious, of course, until she knows the truth and then I think she'll forgive me. I'm pretty sure she will if my plan comes off. The important thing is for *somebody* (I'm not quite sure who yet, but I have an idea) to see how beautifully you dance – so beautifully that they'll know you must go on doing it. That's as far as I've got at the moment. Now, are you ready?' She started the tape. 'Remember how full of joy you are at returning to the world, even as a Wili . . . yes, that's wonderful! . . . Now I'm Albrecht. Don't forget your lilies, and be sure to throw them as you reach the *top* of your jump – it makes you look so much lighter and more ethereal. Like *this*!' Vicki gave a demonstration with a couple of long sprays of Michaelmas daisies; then they went back to the beginning, and Nona tried it for herself. At half-past twelve, they called it a day, as Vicki put it, and went off to bed.

'We must be off early in the morning,' Vicki declared as they said good night outside Jon's room. 'If we're going to hitch-hike, it will take us all our time to get there by Tuesday. We shall have to sleep under haystacks, so let's hope the thunder is only local! Gosh! I've only just thought of something. Those clothes I borrowed from Mrs Hunter!

I meant to ask Mr Hewett to take them back. Well, it may be a week or more before he can do that now, so I'd better write a note to Mrs Hunter explaining matters, and we can post it tomorrow as we go through Keswick.'

Part Three

Chapter 1

On the Road

They crept out of Keswick in the early morning – although 'crept' is hardly the right word, for each of them wore a pair of heavy, nailed hiking boots. (Vicki had managed to find a pair that, when padded with several pairs of socks, fitted Nona tolerably well.) As it was Sunday, there was very little traffic on the roads, and any cars they saw were travelling in the opposite direction.

'They're going to church,' said Vicki. 'Never mind – this afternoon they'll all come out like flies!'

They had decided to go by Carlisle, so their road took them along the eastern shores of Bassenthwaite Lake, and under the shadow of Skiddaw, over whose massive shoulder the sun had not yet risen. The lake lay calm and softly shining in the early morning light, and in the woods the birds twittered sleepily. It was all very fresh and peaceful, 'as if they knew it was Sunday' Vicki said. And then, to add to this feeling, the bell from a little church on the hillside tinkled urgently, and several people came out of the drive of a house nearby, and hurried off up a lane which said 'Millbeck ¼ mile'. None of them took any notice of the two travellers – hikers were too common a sight in Lakeland.

They walked on, and not a single car either met or passed them. At twelve o'clock, they sat down on the grass by the side of the road and opened their rucksacks. They had brought a good supply of food – bread and butter, a tin of luncheon meat (Vicki had even remembered to put in a tin-opener), several bananas, a large slab of fruit cake, a packet of biscuits, and two packets of crisps. Nona's rucksack had a bottle of milk in it, and Vicki's a thermos of hot coffee. They drank the coffee first because it was hot. 'What a pity we could only find one thermos,' said Vicky.

As they sat there, cars in plenty began to put in an appearance, but alas, they were all going in the opposite direction!

'Of course, they're all going into Keswick on this fine Sunday afternoon!' Vicki groaned. 'We might have known! Oh, well – let's walk on. There must be *some* cars going the other way.' And sure enough one appeared as she said the words, but it turned out to be a utility-van full of crates of milk, and the driver intimated by signals that he had no room for them. Presently another car zoomed past, its driver showing very plainly by the rather supercilious expression on her face that hikers came to the Lake District to *walk* didn't they? Well, let them walk!

'She little knows the dire circumstances!' said Vicki. 'What a shock she would get if she knew we were runaways – *you*, anyway! And talking of runaways, I wonder what the Hunters said when they arrived home last night and got our note. Furious wouldn't be the word! I can just imagine the old buffer puffing himself out with righteous indignation, and giving a lecture on the spot to his poor dear better-half about "base ingratitude", and so forth, and so on.'

'I do hope they don't go to the police,' said Nona uneasily.

'Not they!' said Vicki confidently. 'They'll know they were in the wrong to leave you like that, and people who are in the wrong don't fly to the police.'

But here Vicki was mistaken. Major-General Hunter was one of those people who never know (or admit, even to themselves) that they are in the wrong. The first thing he had done when he and his wife arrived back from their dinner party at one o'clock in the morning and found Nona's letter on the kitchen table, was to ring up the Keswick police.

'This girl,' he fumed into the telephone receiver, 'whom we had picked up out of the gutter – well, out of the orphanage, which amounts to the same thing, doesn't it? – this ungrateful girl, to whom my wife and I had shown such kindness, has run away, leaving only this note, which gives us no idea at all as to where she may have gone – oh, yes, she does say Newcastle, I see . . . Why did she run away? Really, I have no idea. One moment please – my wife has just come downstairs, and it appears that the girl is a thief into the bargain. Yes! She has stolen clothing belonging to Mrs Hunter . . . *several* articles, my wife says, including a skirt and jumper. What's that you say – funny articles to pinch? Not at all! She'll sell them, I suppose.'

The police officer at the other end of the wire yawned behind his hand. It was, after all, one o'clock in the morning.

'I understand you and your wife had been away, sir?' he said. 'Could you tell me what time it was when you returned?'

'Oh, it must have been about eleven o'clock,' lied General Hunter glibly.

'It is now one a.m.,' said the police sergeant, who was feeling disgruntled at having been pulled out of his warm bed by the telephone call. 'Why didn't you call us before?'

'Because we've been looking everywhere for the girl,'

answered the General angrily. Really, this policeman was very stupid. 'And now, Sergeant, if you'll just take down the particulars, my wife and I would like to go to bed.'

'Just one moment, sir,' said the policeman. 'How was it the other people in the house didn't see this note you say the girl left on the kitchen table? Had they gone to bed early, or something?'

'*Other* people?' repeated the General. 'There are no other people in the house. My wife and I live alone – we don't take in paying guests!'

'Then this child had been left alone in the house until the late hours, and during a thunderstorm?' There was a note of censure in the man's voice that infuriated General Hunter.

'My good man – how could my wife and I know it was going to thunder?' he exploded. 'If the best you can do is to talk nonsense about thunderstorms, then I bid you *good night!*' He slammed down the receiver, and vented his ill-humour on his wife, who by this time was in bed.

'Really, Helen, it's a disgrace,' he fumed. 'Considering all we pay in rates and taxes, the least the police could do is to be *polite*. That man actually sounded as if he thought we were to blame! It's a scandal!'

'Yes, dear,' said Mrs Hunter with a yawn.

'Well, I hope the Keswick police are more efficient than they sound – that's all!' ranted the General. 'I hope they get on to that girl and bring her back in ignominy and disgrace. It will be our place to teach her where her duty lies. Are you listening, Helen?' But all the answer he got was a gentle snore – Mrs Hunter was already asleep.

At the Keswick police station, the sergeant scratched his head sleepily. Poor little beggar, he thought! Left alone in that house till the early hours. He didn't believe General Hunter's statement about the time he got back from his dinner party, not he! It sounded too fishy! Back at eleven, so he said, and didn't telephone until one in the morning. The police sergeant shrugged his shoulders – he wasn't born yesterday! Well, *he* certainly wouldn't like to be left alone in Rake House at dead of night – leaving the thunderstorm out of it. All those headless statues and things! He was a family man himself, and all his sympathies were with the absconding orphan. Of course, she'd have to be sought after, and found, but for his part he hoped the fire-eating General would be told where to get off – and properly! And as for the child stealing the old so-and-so's wife's jumper and skirt – well, I ask you!

Meanwhile Nona and Vicki had left the Lake District, and were plodding along the highroad towards Carlisle. There was a constant stream of cars, all making for Keswick, but very few travelling the opposite way. However, they were lucky to get several lifts from people who were going short distances in the right direction, and by four o'clock they had covered about half the distance to Carlisle. They sat down on the wide grass verge of the road near a party of picnickers, and ate sandwiches of luncheon meat, washed down with a little coffee they had saved from their lunch, and which was now barely lukewarm.

'Ugh!' said Vicki making a wry face. 'I never knew that tepid coffee was so revolting! . . . Oh, dear! We missed that one!' (A large Ford whizzed by going in the direction of Carlisle.) 'It was nearly empty too. And there goes a police car! Oh, well – I suppose one couldn't very well ask *them* for a lift – it just isn't done!'

Police-sergeant Rice, sitting by the driver of the car, saw the two girls and thought they were with the other picnickers. 'Funny the places people choose to eat their picnics in!' he thought. 'When there are so many beauty spots just round the corner, so to speak, why, in the name of goodness, choose the highroad! Well, I hope the kids' mums and dads see they tidy up afterwards, and take their sandwich papers home with them! Like as not, though, it'll be the mums and dads that'll leave the rubbish!' Never for a minute did he imagine that he had passed within a few feet of the runaway girl he was looking for. To do him justice, Nona had her back to the road, so he didn't see her face.

A few miles further down the road, the two girls got a lift in a car that took them to within eight or nine miles of the city. By this time they were very tired and getting quite footsore.

'I think we'd better call it a day!' Vicki said. 'It's so important that we don't get blisters on our feet. That's one of the snags of being a ballet dancer – one has to be so careful about everything one does. Anyway, as we haven't any money, Carlisle wouldn't really be any use to us if we got there tonight. Our best plan is to find a nice farm, and camp out in their stack-yard.'

They set off down a side road, and very soon a farm came into sight, with the usual collection of outbuildings and a group of straw stacks gleaming golden in the setting sun. They squeezed between two of the stacks, and pulled out some straw. 'We must remember to put it back when we leave,' Vicki said. 'This will do for us to lie on, and there's enough to cover us over. Although it's quite warm now, it's sure to get cold in the middle of the night.

'Ugh!' said Nona. 'It's frightfully tickly, and it's full of spiders. I think I'll do without my quilt after all!'

'You wait till the early morning!' laughed Vicki. 'You'll be only to glad of it then, tickle or not! Here,' (she opened her rucksack) 'how about some more sandwiches? We may as well finish them – they'll be dry by the morning. Luckily, we still have the bananas to eat. Do you have any money at all – I forgot to ask?'

'I've only got one pound and fifty pence left over from my holiday money,' Nona said, ruefully.

'And I've got nothing at all,' said Vicki. 'I wish we had the three pounds I left for that old hag, who didn't deserve it anyway!'

'Yes, and *I* should have paid that,' broke in Nona. 'Some day I'll pay you back.'

'Oh, I didn't mean that,' said Vicki blushing. 'After all, if I hadn't come on the scene, you would never have run away – I mean, not all the way back to Newcastle – so it's *my* responsibility. But the fact remains – we've got just enough to buy some bread rolls and get our flask filled with hot coffee. It should still leave us with a little bit over, too.'

They were both so tired that they fell asleep immediately, and neither of them heard the police car on its return from Carlisle as, having left the main road, it zoomed down the road on the other side of the wall, its head-lamps picking out a gap, and shining on the straw just above their heads.

Chapter 2

Adventure in Carlisle

They slept late next morning. No luxurious mattress or feather bed could have felt more comfortable to the two tired girls than their pile of warm straw. The sun was well up when Vicki yawned and sat up.

'Oh, what a lovely sleep I've had! I don't think I was ever so tired. Nona, wake up! It's nearly ten o'clock!'

Nona came out of her straw like a seal coming up for air. Straw was sticking in her hair, and out of the neck of her dress. Vicki stared at her, and began to laugh. 'I expect I look just as funny!' she giggled. 'We had better have our breakfast first, and then try to tidy ourselves up a bit. We can't go to Carlisle looking like a couple of scarecrows!'

They breakfasted on biscuits, slices of fruit cake, and water from a tap they found in the farmyard nearby. Then they spent some time picking the straw out of each other's hair. 'I feel awfully like a monkey!' Vicki declared. Very soon they felt they were tidy enough to escape notice, so they left the stack-yard (after carefully pushing the loose straw back into the stacks), climbed the fence on to the lane, and made their way back to the highroad. Their rucksacks now hung limply on their shoulders – there was precious little in them except biscuits, bananas, a bottle of milk and an empty thermos.

They managed to get a lift to the outskirts of Carlisle, and by this time they were ravenously hungry – biscuits and a slice of fruit cake aren't exactly filling, as Vicki declared. To add to their discomfort, it had begun to rain

– fine misty rain, exceedingly wetting. They took their mackintoshes out of their rucksacks, and put them on, but the wet got through just the same, and when they reached the city, they were a very bedraggled pair indeed.

'Let's shelter here for a bit,' said Vicki, pushing Nona into the doorway of a shop. 'It may ease off, though it certainly doesn't look like it at the moment. I suppose we're lucky it kept fine last night.' They stood there, shivering and dejected, when suddenly a voice behind them boomed, 'This is the BBC News!'

'Oh, what a fright I got!' exclaimed Vicki. 'I hadn't realized this was a radio shop . . . What's the matter?' Nona had clutched her arm. On the screen of the television set just inside the doorway a face had appeared – Nona's face – and at the same moment the voice said, 'Before I read the news, I have a police notice. The police are anxious to trace the whereabouts of Nona Browning, aged fifteen, reported missing from her home in Keswick since Saturday evening. Will anyone who has seen her, or knows anything about her movements, please contact the police. The missing girl is small for her age, has dark hair and eyes, and has a disfigurement to her face. The child was wearing a print dress and a mackintosh. May be with a companion – sex unknown. Foul play cannot be ruled out—'

Neither Nona nor Vicki waited to hear any more. They fled from the doorway of the radio shop as if pursued by a demon, which indeed they were – the demon of television!

'Oh, I never thought of *that*!' exclaimed Nona.

'It's that beastly man!' exploded Vicki. 'He's just *wanting* to make a fuss. Foul play, indeed! I never heard of anything so ridiculous! Well, that settles it – you'll have to cover your face, and pretend you've got toothache.'

They looked at each other. Finally Nona said, 'Yes, but what with? I haven't got a scarf or anything.'

'Wait a minute.' Vicki went up to a woman who was

looking in a shop window nearby. 'Please,' she said, 'can you tell me where Woolworths is?'

The woman pointed. 'Round the corner, luv, straight down the street towards the station, into the market square, and you'll see it on the right. You look all-in, luv! Is anything the matter?'

'Oh, no – nothing,' Vicki assured her hastily. 'I'm in a hurry, that's all. Thank you ever so much.' She dashed back to Nona. 'Come on! We've some shopping to do.'

They bought a big cotton handkerchief at Woolworths for fifty pence, and Nona tied it round the bottom part of her face. Over the top of it, her great dark eyes looked out sadly. It wasn't hard to imagine she was suffering from toothache! In fact, she got many sympathetic glances from passers-by, and one woman stopped the two of them, and gave them some advice: 'You take your little sister home, luv,' she said to Vicki. 'She looks poorly. You try some kitchen salt in that poor tooth' (to Nona). 'It works like magic! My Bella had ever such a nasty abscess—'

'Oh, thank you,' said Vicki, 'for your advice, I mean. We'll be sure to try it. It's ever so kind of you—' She hurried Nona away, and they walked on down the main street towards the bridge, stopping at a confectioner's to buy some bread rolls. 'And could you fill our thermos with coffee, please?' asked Vicki anxiously.

The woman shook her head.

'You'll have to go to the snack-bar in Cross Street for that,' she said. She came out to the door and gave them directions: 'You cross t'road, and take second turn to the right; then you'd better ask again. Has the little girl got toothache?'

Nona rolled mournful eyes, and Vicki said shamelessly, 'I suppose she ought really to go and have it out, but we keep on hoping it will go off.'

'They never do,' said the woman. 'Take my tip, and have

it out, ducky. Get your sister to take you to Mr Wishart in Gretna Street (you'll pass it on your way to Cross Street). Such a nice man, Mr Wishart – never hurts at all. You ask him to give you gas, and you won't feel nothing at all. Tell him Mrs Anderson sent you. He knows me—'

They managed to get away from the talkative Mrs Anderson at last, and set off across the now crowded street (it was after twelve o'clock by this time) in the direction she had pointed out.

'Gretna Street,' Vicki said, looking up at the sign. 'This is it. Then we're right – I remember Mrs Thingummy-bob mentioning Gretna Street. I think we'd better ask again.' She looked round for a likely person, but before she could stop anyone, Nona clutched her arm.

'Look! Look at that policeman!' Vicki turned and beheld a stout member of the police force staring straight at them. For one agonizing second he stood there, his eyes fixed on them; then he came towards them.

'He's recognized me!' Nona cried in tears. 'Oh, what shall we do?'

'Don't lose your head,' cautioned Vicki. Then, just beside her, she saw a gleaming door-plate:

W. WISHART, DENTL. SURG.
HOURS 9 A.M. – 6 P.M.

Quick as thought she drew Nona inside the doorway. 'That'll fox him!' she said. 'We must wait here for a bit.'

Actually the large policeman hadn't been following them at all – he was merely going home for his lunch, but neither Nona nor Vicki were to know that. They both thought they were being pursued by the Law.

In front of them was a flight of dark stairs. They walked up these, and into a waiting room furnished with the usual table covered with out-of-date magazines, which were being thumbed over by a collection of sad-looking people. A young receptionist came through a door at the far side of the room, notebook in hand, and looked at them enquiringly. 'Have you an appointment?' she asked.

'No,' said Vicki in a broad Cumbrian accent, 'but my little sister has toothache that bad that my mam said to bring her straight away to have t'out. All night long she hollared and yelled fit to bust, and we none of us got a wink of sleep.' If Nona hadn't been so frightened, she would have been amused at Vicki's powers of invention, and her skill with the Cumbrian accent. 'So my dad says, "You tak that kid to t'dentist, and have t'out, and don't come 'ome til'ts done."'

'Well, I'm afraid Mr Wishart is busy with appointments just now,' said the girl. 'He goes for his lunch at one, but if you care to wait until then, perhaps he'll see you for a few minutes. Under the circumstances . . . ' she regarded Nona's muffled face sympathetically. 'We can't very well send away a suffering patient.'

'Oh, thank you ever so much,' said Vicki gratefully. 'Sit down, luv,' to Nona, who was looking more scared every minute. She was wondering if she was really going to lose a tooth!

'Mr Johnson,' said the receptionist, and one of the four people rose and disappeared through the far door.

One after the other the rest of the occupants of the dentist's waiting room rose and disappeared. When the door had closed on the last one, Vicki laid down her year-old copy of *Punch*, and got up.

'Come on!' she said, and taking Nona by the hand, they crept down the dark staircase, and out into the street. To their relief no policeman was waiting for them like a cat at a mouse-hole; in fact, there wasn't a single officer of the law in sight. Vicki breathed a sigh of relief.

'That's put *him* off the scent all right!' she laughed. 'I

wonder what the dentist's receptionist will say when she finds that the birds have flown? She'll probably think you took fright at the last moment!'

Chapter 3

Along the Roman Wall

The rain had stopped by this time, and a watery sun had appeared from behind the clouds. The unexpected stay in the dentist's warm waiting room had dried their clothes, so they felt more cheerful, although they were getting hungrier every minute.

'I think we had better not bother about the coffee,' Vicki said. 'I'll feel easier when we're out of Carlisle. Too many policemen about! Look – there's one over there that I'll swear is eyeing us suspiciously. Thank goodness, he's on point-duty, so he can't come chasing after us!'

They left Carlisle by the bridge over the River Eden, and set off down the Brampton to Newcastle road.

'We must get a lift – or lifts – part of the way at least,' Vicki declared. 'It's much too far to walk all the way – besides, it would take us a week! I'm scared of doing it, though – now that you've been on TV. I feel that everyone will recognize you!'

All went well at first. A lorry driver took them as far as Brampton, and then, after they had walked a mile or two, they heard a car coming up behind them. They stopped and looked round. It was quite a small car, and was being driven very slowly.

'Looks like a woman,' said Vicki. 'Try to look appealing, Nona!' They stood by the side of the road, and when the car was nearly abreast, they signalled to it hopefully. It slowed down, and the driver (Vicki had been right) put her head out of the window:

'I suppose you want a lift?' It wasn't said very graciously, but then Margery Williams wasn't feeling very gracious just then. She was on her way to Haltwhistle to pick up her husband's mother, who had written to say she was coming to stay 'for a week or two' – without as much as a by your leave! Margery couldn't stand her mother-in-law at any time, and the thought of having to 'run about after that old stick', as she put it, for an indefinite period infuriated her. She knew what it would be – old Mrs Williams would go sniffing around the house, finding fault with everything, and never lifting as much as a finger to help. But when Tom came home in the evening, there she would be – turning out the larder, polishing the linoleum, or some such thing, and Tom would say, 'At it again, Mum? Where you get the energy from, old girl, I really don't know! Marvel, isn't she, Marge? You mustn't let her do *too* much, though, or we'll be having her laid up.' Laid up, thought Margery! It would take an earthquake to do that – the old battle-axe was as strong as a horse!

All these thoughts had been chasing each other round in her head when she had spotted the two girls. Oh, well, she thought – they looked tired, and it wouldn't do her any harm to give them a lift.

'Where are you going?' she asked.

'Newcastle,' said Vicki.

'Well, I'm only going as far as Greenhead. I turn off there for Haltwhistle, but if you care for a lift as far as that, you're welcome.' She opened the offside door of the little car. 'Get in!'

'Oh, thank you,' Vicki said gratefully. She motioned Nona into the back seat, and took the front one herself. 'It's awfully good of you.'

'You're welcome,' Margery Williams said again. They drove for a long time in silence. Margery Williams' thoughts returned to the vexed question of her mother-in-law, and

Vicki's and Nona's to the long journey still in front of them. They were doing well, but would they be there in time?

'You're very *young*, aren't you, to be hitch-hiking all by yourselves?' said Mrs Williams at length, dragging her thoughts away from Tom's mother.

'I'm older than I look,' Vicki assured her. 'I'm seventeen, and my sister is fifteen. We're really quite old enough to look after ourselves.'

Margery Williams, taking a sidelong glance at Vicki sitting beside her, and another at Nona by means of her driving-mirror, said doubtfully, 'Well, I *hope* so! I don't altogether agree with it.'

It was when they were within a couple of miles of Greenhead, that the awful thing happened. Mrs Williams, who had been studying Nona covertly, said suddenly, 'What's the matter with your face, little girl?'

Nona's eyes widened in alarm, and the colour flooded into her pale cheeks, but Vicki kept her head. 'My sister's got toothache,' she said.

'Oh,' said Mrs Williams, 'then why doesn't she get it out?'

'We did go to the dentist today in Carlisle,' said Vicki truthfully, 'but he was too busy to see her.'

Margery Williams clicked her tongue sympathetically. 'Shame!' she said. 'I thought they were compelled by law to take out a tooth if it was aching really hard. Oh, well, you'll just have to go again tomorrow when you get to Newcastle. And mind you *do*; it's no use putting off the evil day where an aching tooth is concerned. It *was* Newcastle you said you were going to, wasn't it? Well, I must say it seems queer to me for two children like you to be hitch-hiking all that way . . . My gracious! I've just thought of something! Oh, thank goodness, there's a telephone box. You two sit still – I shan't be long.' She parked the car in the lay-by where the telephone box was situated, and took some money out of her handbag.

'She's gone to ring up the police!' said Nona in terror. 'She's guessed! I knew it the moment she said that about my face – she's been watching me through the mirror.'

'It certainly looks like it,' agreed Vicki. 'We must get out of here.' They waited until the telephone box had engulfed Mrs Williams, then they shot out of the car, and fled for their lives. There happened to be a small copse of fir trees near the road, and they dived into its sweet scented depths, and flung themselves down on the pine needles. They were now quite hidden from the road.

Vicki breathed a sigh of relief. 'We aren't caught *yet*,' she said.

Meanwhile, in the telephone box Margery Williams was ringing up her sister, who lived in the same street.

'Ethel! Is that you, Ethel? . . . Thank goodness you're there! My dear, I've done the most ghastly thing . . . Yes, I know, but this really *is* ghastly. I've put the joint in the oven, and forgotten to turn down the heat. It'll be burnt to a cinder by the time I get back, and Tom's mother will be with me . . . Yes, she's invited herself! . . . Thank you – I expect I'll need it. Well, look Ethel, could you be an angel and pop in and see to it – the joint, I mean. Oh, and you'd better turn the gas out altogether, just in case . . . The key? In the usual place, under the flower-pot on the kitchen window-sill. Thanks ever so! Do the same for you one day . . . What's that? Where am I? Well, I'm at Greenhead – actually a couple of miles this side. Got two kids in the car – hitch-hiking to Newcastle if you please. Really, the things folks let their kids get up to nowadays, but of course it's none of *my* business . . . There go the pips! Bye-bye, then. See you tomorrow!' She hung up the receiver, picked up her handbag, and left the telephone box. Well, she'd certainly been lucky this time! Whew! How ghastly if they'd got back to find the house filled with the stench of burning mutton! She'd never have heard the last of it!

At the thought of her narrow escape, all her good humour returned. She even had a mind to go out of her way to give these kids a bit of a break. She needn't take the Haltwhistle road at Greenhead – she could take a side road further on, and that would put the children a mile or two further on their way.

But when she got back to the car, it was empty. She looked round vaguely to see if they were having a walk round the lay-by to stretch their legs, but no. Neither was there any sign of them on the road ahead, or, for that matter, on the road behind either. Their rucksacks had gone too. Mrs Williams blinked her eyes in amazement. It was almost as if she'd imagined them – they'd vanished into thin air!

Nona and Vicki crouched in the undergrowth at the edge of the little wood and watched the proceedings with fast beating hearts.

'She's wondering what to do now,' said Vicki. 'Whether to wait for the police to come, or to drive on. If she decides to stay here, we're in a spot, because if we come out on to the road ahead, she's bound to see us, and even if we managed to get over the brow of the hill without her seeing us, she could easily come up behind and catch us.'

Their fears proved to be ungrounded, however. After looking around vaguely for a minute or two, and giving some rather half-hearted 'hullos', Mrs Williams got back into her car, and drove away. Actually she had decided that a car must have come up while she was in the telephone box, and that the two girls had got a lift with its driver. 'Really, the modern generation!' she said aloud as she let in the clutch. 'No manners at all! And no patience! Why, I wasn't more than five minutes.'

Vicki and Nona waited until the car had disappeared into the distance, and then came out from their hiding place.

'The question is,' said Vicki as they walked down the road towards Greenhead, 'how long will it take for the police to get here? Not long I should say. They have very fast cars. I wonder if she rang up Brampton, or Greenhead? We had better hide every time we hear a car coming in either direction.'

Of course, as soon as they had taken this decision, vehicles appeared like magic – cars, lorries, motorbikes, scooters, and even a caravan.

'Maddening, isn't it?' Vicki declared. 'I expect any of them would be perfectly safe, but we simply daren't risk it. Even if we stopped one, and it *was* OK, a police car might overtake it and see us, and we'd be properly caught. While we're on our own feet, we can at least hide.'

'Do you think we're going to get there in time?' Nona asked anxiously. 'Newcastle still seems an awful long way off.'

'Oh, don't be so cheerful!' Vicki answered sarcastically, although Nona had only put into words the fear that lay in her own heart.

They climbed over the drystone wall that bounded the road on either side, and safely hidden behind it, and sheltered from the cold wind, they sat and ate the last of the bread rolls, and the last two bananas. They had finished their milk long ago, so they drank a mouthful or two of water from a spring that gushed out of a wall and fell into a green mossy trough below.

'I know it's all wrong,' said Vicki, 'and one runs a danger of catching typhoid, and goodness only knows what, but there *are* times . . . ' She dug a small hole in the turf, and carefully buried the banana skins. Then they both stood up, and hunched on their rucksacks again; after which they climbed back on to the road. They had walked about half a mile when they heard a vehicle coming up behind them.

'Look out! Here comes a car!' They dived through a gateway and hid behind the obliging wall, while the car shot past.

'Only an innocent-looking woman!' sighed Vicki. 'Oh, dear – if only one *knew*! . . . And I do believe it's going to rain again.'

The road stretched in front of them, disappearing into the distance in a series of switchbacks. Parallel with it, first on one side, and then on the other, ran a deep, wide ditch filled with foxgloves and meadowsweet. Sometimes there were two ditches.

'One of them is the *vallum*,' explained Vicki, 'and the other is the *fosse*. Papa has explained them to me several times, but I *never* can remember which is which. They were made by the Romans as boundary lines, to show where Roman Britain ended, and where the Barbarians (that was *us*) began. The vallum was also a fortification. Filled with bits of swords and spears stuck in the wrong way up, they must have been pretty fierce! . . . Oh, look – there's the Roman Wall!' Over hills and valleys, seeming to enjoy overcoming obstacles in the shape of black crags, and hilly knolls, the Wall snaked its way towards Newcastle. Sometimes (usually when it approached a lonely farm house) it tailed off, and got lost in the gorse and heather.

'They've used the stones to build their pigsties with, I expect!' laughed Vicki. 'Most of the buildings round here are made of Roman stones – cheaper than quarrying new ones!'

The rain had stopped again, but as they climbed higher, they found themselves enveloped in thick cloud. In a way, as Vicki said, it made things easier. If all they could see of a car were its sidelights dimly shining through the gloom, it certainly couldn't see *them*! Mile after weary mile they plodded on, stopping now and then to rest their aching feet. As the afternoon wore on, the fog thickened, and it grew darker, until only the white line down the middle of the road kept them from staggering off it on to the wide verge of hummocky grass.

A building loomed out of the mist on their right, and at the same moment the headlights of a car which was evidently just leaving the building fell upon a sign swinging above the door.

TWICE BREWED

'Oh, it's the Twice Brewed Inn!' exclaimed Vicki. 'We're further on than I thought.' She looked after the glowing tail-lights of the car and thought with a pain at her heart: 'That was a sports car just like Jon's. It's a new one – he got it for his birthday. I wonder where Jon is now?'

'Do you think we could go in and get a cup of tea, or something?' Nona's voice broke in upon her thoughts. The younger girl was chilled to the bone, and her feet were aching; also the amber lamplight from the inn parlour beckoned invitingly. 'Do let's!'

But Vicki wouldn't hear of it. 'Sorry, but it's too dangerous. They've got the telephone, you see,' (she pointed to the wires overhead) 'and the police are sure to have alerted them. We'd just be walking into a trap. We must walk on a little further – just another mile or two – and then I think I know where we can get shelter.'

Nona didn't argue. After all, it was for *her* this awful trek through the night, this race against time. She was full of gratitude towards this new friend, who was going without food, and enduring all manner of hardship, just so that she, obscure Nona Browning, should get her chance to become a dancer. What she didn't realize was that Vicki, spoilt only child of famous parents, was enjoying herself hugely! To

Nona, being hungry and footsore was nothing out of the ordinary. But Vicki Scott had never been hungry in her life. Always, she had only had to ask for whatever she wanted, and it had been given to her. And now, this pitting of her strength against the forces of nature was something quite new to her, and she thrilled to it like a mountaineer overcoming an unknown and dangerous peak.

Chapter 4

The Roman Camp

It was fortunate, perhaps, that they could not see the road in front of them. Mile after undulating mile, it stretched ahead, and even Vicki might have been daunted. As it was, they could only see a few yards to each side and in front of them. As they reached the top of each switchback, the mist thickened, and then thinned out when they went down the other side. They seemed to be in a deserted world; they didn't meet a single pedestrian, and they had only seen the one car since they had left Greenhead. It was evident that even the police had stayed at home!

At one point, the road suddenly widened at their left-hand side, and here Vicki stopped. 'This may be what I've been looking for,' she declared. A sign-post, barely discernible, pointed over the mist enshrouded fields:

HOUSESTEADS (BORCOVICIUM) ROMAN CAMP
National Monument

'Yes, this is it,' she added. 'Here is where we leave the road.'

'Is – is it very far?' asked Nona faintly, and then Vicki noticed how white she had become, and that she was beginning to limp.

'Oh, I'm so sorry,' she said, conscience-stricken. 'I ought to have seen. You're nearly all-in! I keep forgetting how strong I am – in spite of being so small. Oh, well, it's not much further – I mean to the place where we're going to spend the night (if we're lucky!), and it's over soft turf, so that ought to help. Here, give me your rucksack, and lean on my arm. We simply *must* find somewhere to sleep, and I think I know a place.'

There appeared to be a rough but well-worn track over the short turf, and obviously Vicki knew it well. The two of them staggered along it, Nona leaning heavily on Vicki's arm. At first the path went downhill, then through a small gate, and up the other side of a fairly steep slope. On either side, strange outcrops of rock (or were they the remains of human dwellings?) stuck out of the grass.

'It's all part of the Roman Camp,' Vicki explained. 'These places – outside the actual walls – were the civil dwellings – shops, houses, places of entertainment, and so on. That square enclosure over there is called the "Murder House", because several skeletons of women were found in it when they were digging it out. Well, here is the south gate, and over there is the hut where the National Trust man sits during the daytime to collect people's money. I only hope we can get in.'

They were lucky. The door of the hut was locked, but the window was open, and Vicki managed to push the bottom part up.

'We may as well go the whole hog, and add "breaking and entering" to our other crimes!' she laughed. 'I think we've every excuse – especially *you*, Nona. I can always say we did it in a desperate effort to preserve life – *your* life! It isn't far from the truth,' she added, taking an anxious look at her exhausted companion. 'You stay here, and I'll squeeze in and open the door from inside. Fortunately it's a Yale lock.'

In a very few minutes, she reappeared at the door.

'We're in luck!' she said triumphantly. 'There's even a camp-bed!'

The door-keeper of the Roman Camp had done himself

well. There was an oil-stove, which evidently heated the hut, and on the top of which you could boil a kettle. A box of matches stood beside it, and the kettle, half full of water, was standing on the floor. In an orange-box in one corner was a plate with butter on it, a box of tea and a tin half full of sweetened condensed milk.

'Oh, well,' said Vicki, pulling a wry face. 'I suppose he wasn't to know I don't take sugar in my tea! I shall just have to put up with it! Now if only we had some bread, we'd be able to have a real meal . . . Oh, look!' She had been rummaging in a small cupboard nailed to the wall of the hut, and now she held up the end of a small loaf of bread, and a tin of baked beans. 'We're certainly in luck!'

By this time it was quite dark outside but the oil-stove had a panel of red mica in front that cast a warm glow through the hut, and Vicki had found a candle stuck in a bottle, so they were very cosy. Nona had collapsed on to the camp-bed, but now the warmth began to revive her, and the colour had come back into her pale cheeks.

'I'm wonderfully warm now,' she said, snuggling under the old tartan rug that covered the camp-bed, 'but I feel awful, letting you do everything.'

'You stay there, and rest your precious feet,' ordered Vicki. 'I'll do the cooking, and you can help with the washing-up – always provided we can find some water to do it in – I think I can hear a stream outside.'

Before they began to eat their meal, Vicki went out of the hut and, by the light of an electric torch she had found in the cupboard, she picked out the glint of water. A few minutes later she returned with a full kettle, which she set on the top of the oil-stove to heat while they ate.

'Oh, what a wonderful meal!' she said with a sigh of happiness. 'Baked beans and potato crisps,' (they had found half a packet at the bottom of Nona's rucksack), 'bread and butter – and, of course, hot tea. Here's a toast to Mr

Whatever-his-name-is! May his customers multiply, although I don't expect that benefits him personally, unless they tip him.

They drank Vicki's toast to the absent custodian of the Roman Camp; after which they washed up, leaving enough water in the kettle to wash themselves too, and then they snuggled down on the camp-bed, side by side, covered by the tartan rug, and fell asleep immediately.

Outside, the mist rolled in billowing clouds; a dog fox called to his mate in a succession of eerie howls. She answered him from the ruins, standing on the remains of a Roman centurion's house to do so, and throwing up her head to the sliver of moon, which had suddenly appeared in a rift of the clouds. If the ghosts of the Roman Legions were abroad that night, they did not disturb the sleeping girls.

Chapter 5

More Trouble

It was dawn when Vicki woke, and for a moment she couldn't imagine where she was. Then she remembered – of course, the Roman Camp at Housesteads! And then she was aware of a strange rushing, tearing sound – rather like that of a rough sea. It shook and hurled itself against the hut like a dog shaking a rat. Vicki threw back her portion of the rug, and ran to the door. The mist had vanished, and the wind had risen to a gale. Clouds scudded across a slate-grey sky, and a spatter of raindrops, like a handful of lead shot, was flung in her face. A small plantation of stunted fir trees nearby was almost laid flat by the fury of the gale.

Nona was still asleep, but Vicki shook her awake.

'We must get away before His Nibs comes back,' she declared. 'He mustn't find us here. Although we haven't actually done any harm, still he's sure to ask dozens of awkward questions. I'll put the kettle on and we'll have a cup of tea before we go, and eat the rest of the bread. I'll fill the thermos, too, while I'm about it.'

They left the hut clean and tidy, and Vicki wrote a note and propped it against the oil-stove. It said:

Two benighted hikers were forced to break into your hut, and shelter there for the night, and very glad they were of it, I can tell you! They ate a tin of baked beans, some butter, bread (pretty stale), and a little tea, and leave sixty pence for same, and hope it is enough. It's all we've got!

Yours sincerely, TWO HIKERS

The gale was almost worse than the mist. It seized them in its teeth the moment they left the hut, and tore at their faces like a savage animal. It howled round their ears, whipped their mackintoshes against their legs, and stung their faces like a whiplash. It was impossible to speak, impossible to hear if speaking had been possible; it was almost impossible to think! The road stretched away into infinity, and the Wall, running by its side, only left it to take in some frowning black crag, or to skirt a grey, reed-encircled tarn, or to lose itself in the out-buildings of some lonely farmhouse. Vicki noticed, not for the first time, that these buildings all had their backs turned to the cold inhospitable north, and their windows looking out hopefully towards the warm south. She tried to point this out to Nona, but was quite unable to make herself heard.

The day passed, and still they walked on. Whenever a car appeared, either in front or behind, they hid. It was made more difficult because of the wind that effectively drowned the sound of approaching traffic. They had long since drunk their thermos of tea, and now they were both cold and hungry. Nona's face was pinched and white and Vicki, taking a sidelong look at her when she thought she wasn't looking, began to wonder at the wisdom of what she had done. What if her plan should come to nothing in the end? What would happen to Nona? She consoled herself with the thought that Nona couldn't be worse off than she had been before – unless of course she was sent back to the Hunters. General Hunter, thought Vicki, would most certainly take it out on her. However, she didn't think it likely. The authorities, she felt sure, would take a poor view of the Hunters' behaviour in leaving a child of Nona's age alone in Rake House on her first night there. Anyway, thought Vicki, her father (her heart swelled with pride at the thought of her dramatic father) would settle everything.

But at the moment it was a question as to whether Nona would be able to stand the journey, and (more important still) whether she would be fit to dance next day. If only they hadn't been pursued by the police, everything would have been easy. Since they had left Housesteads, four cars had passed them, and three of them were empty except for the driver.

'Want a lift, miss?' cried a voice, just heard above the wind.

Vicki jumped with fright. A tractor drawing a hay-bogy behind it had suddenly shot out of a nearby gateway (unheard, because of the wind) and its driver, a lad of about sixteen, with a shock of hair blowing in the gale, was leaning out of his seat towards her in his endeavour to shout above the hurricane. Vicki thought quickly. After all – a hay-bogy was safe enough – the police weren't likely to ring up all the farmers; on the other hand, it *might* be a trap. She decided to risk it.

'Come on, Nona!' she shouted, and half pushed the younger girl on to a pile of sweet smelling bales of hay. 'Thank you!' she shouted to the farm-hand. 'How far are you going?'

'The other side of Chollerford, miss,' he shouted back. 'To a farm nearby. Heard of Hunter's Crag, miss?'

'Of course I have,' shouted Vicki. 'You mean Jack Dillon's place? He's a great friend of my father's.'

'Is he now? Well, me dad works for'm. Nice canny man, Jack Dillon.'

The conversation languished, partly because Vicki didn't want the lad to start asking awkward questions as to who she was and how she came to know the local farmers, but chiefly because it was almost impossible to shout against the wind. She was quite sure now that the young man had nothing to do with the police.

The two girls lay sprawled full-length on the bogy, half

hidden by the bales of hay, and also sheltered from the full force of the wind. Nona was half asleep, but Vicki kept watching for a pursuing police car. Every time a vehicle approached, she pulled the hay over herself and her companion, so that they wouldn't be seen. It had stopped raining, but the wind still howled.

'Well, miss – here you are!' Vicki had almost fallen asleep herself, and the boy's voice jerked her awake. They had drawn in to a gateway by the side of the road, and she could see a stony cart-track leading to a distant farmhouse, half hidden behind a windbreak of fir trees. Although Vicki didn't know it, it was here, in this very field, that her father and mother had left their ponies on their ride through the mist to catch the London train.

'I hope you get to where you're making for, miss,' the boy was saying. 'Where did you say it was?'

Vicki hadn't told him as a matter of fact, but it didn't seem to matter, now that they were so near the end of their journey.

'We're going to Newcastle,' she said, 'and we must be there tonight.'

The youth whistled, and looked at Nona.

'The little girl looks all-in,' he remarked. 'You'll have to get some more lifts, or you'll never make it.'

'Oh, we'll manage somehow,' Vicki assured him, adding to herself, 'We'll *have* to! Well, good-bye, and thank you so much for the lift. You have no idea what a help it was.'

'You're welcome, miss,' said the boy with a grin. He was properly taken with Vicki. A game girl if ever he saw one! He had no idea, of course, how far the two of them had travelled. Carlisle would have been his guess. He would have been very astonished if he had known they had come all the way from Keswick, sleeping out for a couple of nights into the bargain!

*

They staggered up Brunton Bank, coming out into the wind again when they reached the open moor. Behind them they could hear a car grinding up the steep hill in bottom gear.

'A bakery-van!' exclaimed Vicki, looking round. 'That ought to be safe enough!'

They signalled to the van, and it stopped. A man's head poked out of the door: 'Want a lift?'

'Oh, please – desperately. How far are you going?'

'Stagshaw road-ends,' said the man. 'Turn off there for Corbridge.'

'Even just that far will be a great help,' Vicki assured him. 'My little sister is *so* tired, and so hungry too.' (She was thinking of all the loaves of bread in the back of the van.) 'Get in, Nona.'

'Wait a minute,' said the van driver. 'Hungry did you say? Would you say "no" to a couple of teacakes? Mind you they're a bit stale, by now, but you're welcome.'

'I should just say we wouldn't!'

'Half a tick, then.' The man jumped down from the driving-seat, went round to the back of his van, and returned with the teacakes. 'Here you are then. Wish I had some more, but them's the last two.'

'They've saved our lives!' Vicki declared passing one of the teacakes to Nona. They sat squeezed, three abreast in the front seat of the van and the miles fled away.

'We'll do it yet!' Vicki said softly. The man turned to her.

'What's that you say? Can't hear for the wind.'

'I was just talking to myself,' Vicki shouted.

He looked at her severely, half turning in the driving-seat to do so. 'Don't do that, miss,' he said seriously. 'My mam allus says it's the first sign of lunacy!'

They watched the baker's van disappear down the

Corbridge road with regret. It had been a very comfortable few miles, and there was no other vehicle in sight.

'If a private car shows up, I think we'll risk it,' Vicki said, looking anxiously at Nona. 'I'm getting reckless! It's odd that we haven't seen a single police car.' As they passed the garage at the cross-roads, a young man who was doing something to one of the petrol-pumps stared at them curiously. 'You don't suppose . . . ' Vicki said to Nona in alarm. But the man bent again to his work, and showed no sign of rushing inside to the telephone. 'I expect we *do* look a couple of sketches – after two nights out – enough to make anyone stare!'

Their next lift was in a battered old Ford very long past its prime, but it was a godsend to the exhausted travellers. They flew along at twenty-five miles an hour, and felt as if they were doing seventy! The driver, a university student, was just returning from a climbing holiday in Scotland, and the back of the car was full of camping gear. Vicki perched herself on top of a couple of huge rucksacks, with a primus-stove for a back-rest, while Nona sat on a tent.

'Sorry the front seat's full up,' the young climber apologized, and indeed it was. Three suitcases were piled one on top of the other, besides several pairs of huge nailed boots, and three or four coils of rope. 'I hope you can manage in the back there. If you look about a bit, you might find a sleeping-bag. It would make the seat a bit softer!'

'I've already found it, thank you,' Vicki laughed. They sat in silence for a bit, then she said, 'What a lot of pairs of boots you have! Do you wear them in turns?'

The young man laughed.

'Oh, they're not all mine! They belong to my friends. They pushed their stuff in here for me to bring home, while they had a couple of days in Edinburgh.'

'I see,' said Vicki. 'By the way, are you going right into Newcastle?'

'As far as Denton. My mother lives there. That won't leave you far to go – couple of miles at the most, and you can get a bus into town from there.'

Vicki thought of their financial situation, and said nothing to this. There was silence again; then the young man burst out, 'I say, you two *have* got some money between you, I suppose – I mean enough to get you into Newcastle by bus?'

'Not a sou,' said Vicki cheerfully.

He put his left hand in his pocket, and pulled out a handful of coins.

'See what you can find there. The bus is about forty pence each, but you better take a couple of quid. I can't let you have more, because I'm nearly on the rocks myself. Let me have it back later, if you can.'

'I promise,' said Vicki seriously, helping herself to some coins. 'And thank you.' The money would just save them, she thought. She had been wondering what they would do when they reached the city. Telephone calls cost money – she had quite forgotten that, when she had left every penny they had in the caretaker's hut at Housesteads. Of course, she could always ring up her home at Bracken, and reverse the charge, but that would mean waiting hours till a car arrived to pick them up. And then there was Nona. She wanted to keep Nona quite secret – the success of her plan depended upon that. Anyway, the matter was settled now. There would be enough money left over from their bus fare to ring up her friends and arrange a bed for herself and Nona for the night. She was full of gratitude to the young undergraduate. She'd see he got his money back all right!

And then, just when victory seemed to be in their grasp, the awful thing happened. There seemed to be something going on at the bus stop which the young man had pointed out – there were several cars lined up, and a crowd of people watching.

'It's a traffic-block,' said Nona. Now that she was on home ground, she had perked up, and was looking quite cheerful. 'My! What a huge furniture-van! Someone's moving house. The bus'll never get past all that lot!'

There was a lot of shouting on the part of the bus driver, and manoeuvring on the part of the driver of the van. And then a policeman appeared from nowhere and took command of the situation. He watched the furniture-van back inch by inch towards a house, where various bits of furniture – looking very naked as furniture does when out of doors – stood waiting to be loaded into the van. One by one they were draped in sacking and whisked away by a couple of hefty removal men wearing green baize aprons. And then, at one and the same time, three things happened – the bus, which had disentangled itself from the cars, pinged its bell as a warning to intending passengers that it was about to start; an especially lively gust of wind caught Nona's scarf and whirled it away, and the policeman turned round and saw her. It was obvious that he had heard the description of the missing girl, or had seen her picture on television.

'Hey, you two!' he shouted.

Vicki and Nona dashed towards the bus, but it moved off when they were still a few yards away. 'Quick, round here!' They squeezed between the van and the wall, and then into the house where the removal was going on. The two men were still in the van, arranging the pieces of furniture they had just brought out of the house, but a third was coming down the stairs. He gave a whistle of surprise when he saw the two girls. 'Well, of all the . . . ! Why, it's Nona Browning!'

At first Nona, coming out of the light, didn't see who it

was. Then she gave a cry. 'Why, it's Jude! I can't believe it! I thought you were driving a van, or something.'

'So I am – *this* van,' he nodded towards the pantechnicon.

'Oh, Jude – you must help us,' she said, urgently. It was Nona who took command now. 'The police are after us.'

'The police?' The young man (Vicki saw that he was really only a boy, although he was so tall and strong) hustled them into a back room. 'What's all this about?' he said sternly. 'What do you mean by saying the police are after you?'

'Oh, we – I – haven't done anything wrong – not really wrong, Jude,' Nona assured him. 'I ran away, that's all, but my picture was on TV and that policeman outside recognized me.'

'The dickens he did!' exclaimed Jude. 'Where is he now? Did he see you come in here?'

'I don't think so.'

'You stay in here – both of you,' ordered Jude, 'and I'll go and find out.' He strode to the door and looked about him, trying to appear unconcerned. The policeman was standing a few yards away, looking puzzled.

'Seems it's going to rain, officer,' said Jude innocently. 'Good job we've about finished. Looks as if we're in for a proper storm.'

'It does that,' said the policeman. 'By the way, seen a couple of kids anywhere about?'

'Coupla kids?' Jude scratched his head. 'Just them two that got on the bus.'

'Are you sure they got on the bus?' questioned the policeman. 'I'd have sworn it went off without them. I thought myself they went in here somewhere.'

'Nope. Saw 'em get on the bus,' insisted Jude. 'You'd better hop on the next one, officer, if you want to catch 'em.'

'OK, I will,' said the policeman. 'There won't be another

for ten minutes though, so meantime I'll just be taking a look round in here.'

'Please yourself,' said Jude nonchalantly. 'Take a dekko in the garage, while you're about it, officer. They might have nipped in there while we weren't looking. Good place to hide in.'

Having seen the man on his way to the garage, Jude went back indoors. 'Quick! In here!' he said to Vicki, opening the lid of a large oak blanket-box that stood in the hall, and emptying its contents (a sofa-rug, and three pink satin cushions, heavily ruched) on to the floor. 'I'll get them to carry it out to the van next, then you can hide behind the furniture that's already in there.' He closed the lid and turned to Nona. 'Think you can squeeze into this tea-chest – you're small? It'll only be for a few minutes.'

Nona curled up inside the chest, and Jude covered her with newspaper, and on top of that, he laid two large ornamental plates that had been hanging on the wall of the living-room.

'China!' he said to no one in particular. Then he went back to Vicki, and covered her with a layer of fat volumes of the *Encyclopaedia Britannica*, which were standing alongside, waiting to be packed. He wasn't a minute too soon. As he closed the lid, footsteps sounded in the hall.

'That you, Bert?' said Jude. 'Give us a hand with these chests will you, and keep 'em the right way up. This one's full of china.'

'Some china!' grunted Bert. 'Must be some special kind – made of lead! Or maybe a dead body or two – like in them who-dunnits my missis is so keen on. Righty-ho! Shove it along this way.' They pushed the tea-chest up the ramp, and into the back of the van, and went back for the blanket-box.

'Books in this,' said Jude. '*Encyclopaedia Britannica*! They weigh a ton, and I'd like to bet no one ever reads 'em. Well, I ask you, chum – who *would*? Get a move on, Bert!'

Half-way down the garden path they met the policeman returning from his fruitless search of the garage.

'What's that you've got there?' he demanded. 'It looks heavy.'

'It sure is, officer, it's books!' said Jude, putting down his end of the box and mopping his brow. 'Complete set of *Encyclopaedia Britannica*. Just your line, what! Win all them quiz competitions with these – except for just one thing. They're a wee bit out of date – 1914.' He raised the lid a fraction, and patted one of the volumes. 'Crikey! The things some people hang on to. Wouldn't be me! Say, did you find those two kids you were looking for yet?'

'Not yet,' said the policeman. 'I'm beginning to think you were right, and they must have got on that bus.'

'Told you so, officer!' shouted Jude over his shoulder, as he and Bert staggered towards the van. 'But you go on looking. Several built-in wardrobes upstairs. Take a look inside them – never know what you might find! Mrs Thingummy's fur coat, most likely,' he added, under his breath to Bert. 'Push it in alongside the other one, chum.' They slid the blanket-box into position, and looked round.

'Just about full,' said Bert. 'Might manage the settee of the three-piece suite.'

'Right-ho,' agreed Jude. 'It'll go in front – with a bit of luck.'

When Bert had gone back to the house, Jude raised the lid of the blanket-box, removed a couple of volumes of the *Encyclopaedia Britannica* and surveyed Vicki looking back at him with admiring eyes. 'Oh, you were marvellous!' she declared. 'I don't wonder Nona thinks a lot of you.'

'I didn't know she did,' he said with a grin. 'You all right, kid?' He raised the lid of the tea-chest, and looked down at Nona anxiously. She was pale, and not nearly so cock-a-hoop as Vicki. 'You'd better wait till we've started; then you can come out and hide behind that wardrobe. Don't let Bert see you, though. Not that he isn't OK, but the fewer people who know about you, the better. I'll have to think of some yarn to tell him so's I can stop somewhere to let you out.' He shut the lid down on Vicki, and replaced the newspapers on top of the tea-chest, and was gone. A few minutes later, they heard the ramp being raised, the double doors slammed, and the furniture-van rumbled away.

Vicki and Nona came out of their respective hiding-places, and after stretching their legs, sat down, side by side, behind the wardrobe. The van rumbled on for some time, and then, just when they were wondering if it was ever going to stop, it drew up and Jude put his head in at the door.

'You'd better hop out here,' he said. 'I've sent Bert off to get some fags. The house we're going to is just round the corner, and they might ask questions if you two kids were unshipped with their furniture!'

'Where exactly are we?' Vicki wanted to know.

'Jesmond – Manor Drive,' said Jude. 'Know it?'

Vicki shook her head, but Nona exclaimed, 'Oh, yes, I know it – it's not so very far from where I used to go to school. Quite near Mary Martin's as well, and that's where we want to be, isn't it?' She appealed to Vicki.

'Yes – but not tonight. We've got to find somewhere to sleep first.'

'You mean you two kids have got nowhere to go?' said Jude.

'Not yet,' said Vicki, 'but I have several friends living in Newcastle – it's just a case of catching them in. I shall ring them up one by one, until I find someone who can give us a bed.'

'You could doss down in my digs,' said Jude somewhat tentatively. He was rather overawed by Vicki. Not his class, as he would have put it. 'Mrs Spraggan has a camp-bed going begging in her attic for one of you, and the other one could have mine. I could sleep on the settee in the lounge – I've done it before when she had her in-laws to stay.'

Vicki considered the matter.

'Well – it *would* save a lot of trouble – if you're sure you don't mind —'

'OK – that's settled then. You run along, the two of you before Bert gets back, and tell Ma Spraggan I sent you. She'll fix you up.' He hustled them out of the van.

'Yes, but what address?'

Jude grinned. 'Suffering cats!' he exclaimed. 'If it isn't just about where we've come from – 36, Denton Drive! If that doesn't beat cock fighting! Oh, well – you've shaken off the police, and you can get a bus. Got some money, kid?' He turned to Vicki.

'Enough for that,' she answered.

'So long, then,' said Jude. 'See you later. Keep your face covered,' he added to Nona. 'It sort of gives you away.'

Chapter 6

Explanations

That night Vicki slipped out of 36, Denton Drive and rang her home, Bracken Hall.

'Who is that speaking? Oh, you, Trixie! . . . Yes, of *course* I'm all right. Why shouldn't I be? . . . I don't know what you mean . . . Look, Trixie, can I speak to Papa? . . . Yes, *now*, this minute . . . Well, can't you keep his coffee hot while I talk to him? Oh, *thank* you, darling, Trixie! Please be quick and find him – it's very important!'

While she waited with the receiver at her ear, Vicki amused herself by drawing caricatures of ballet dancers all round the telephone directory (which, incidentally, were to prove a source of great amusement to subsequent users of the kiosk!). Everything was working out splendidly, she thought. She had left Nona tucked up in bed and asleep. Now there was only one last hurdle to clear, and with the help of her papa, she would clear it.

'Hullo! Is that Papa? This is Vicki – I'm so sorry I had to reverse the charges, but I was short of small change.' (So she was, and of big change too!) 'Look, Papa – will you do something for me? . . . yes, I know, but don't make rash promises until you hear what it is – it may be difficult. Is Mama there? Oh, *good*! I was so afraid she didn't arrive till tomorrow, and that might have been too late . . . yes, I'll explain after. The point is, could you come to the dress rehearsal at Mary's tomorrow, and bring Mama with you? . . . Yes, of course I know it's unusual, especially as she's the Guest of Honour at the Show the next day, but I have my reasons, and after all nobody will know except Mary and the kids. Anyway, I want her there. I *must* have her there! Please, *please*, Papa! Tell her I want her opinion about the way I throw my lilies – or the way I disappear back into my grave at the end of the ballet – or – or any old thing! I'm sure *you* can think up something convincing, Papa.'

'I expect I can,' said Sebastian drily. 'I wish I knew what was behind all this, Vicki.'

'You'll know tomorrow,' she promised. 'Until then, good-bye. I must go now, and get some sleep . . . oh, yes, I didn't sleep awfully well last night, as a matter of fact. Why? Oh, short of bedclothes! Where? I'll tell you that as well, when I see you and Mama tomorrow at the dress rehearsal – two o'clock, sharp! Good night, darling Papa! . . . What's that? Oh, I'm dossing down – I mean putting up – with a friend at 36, Denton Drive. No, it's no one *you* know . . . Ring up Jon? Oh, *must* you? I don't think he'll be a bit interested – he went off and left me high and dry at Keswick. It was very awkward, because I was short of money . . . You mean he went back there? Well, that explains what Trixie meant . . . Anyway, good-bye, Papa – your coffee will be getting cold!'

Vicki went back to her camp-bed in Mrs Spraggan's attic with an easy mind. She was quite sure, now that she had contacted her all-powerful father, that her plan for Nona would succeed.

Next morning Nona, who was sleeping in Jude's little room over the front-door, was awakened by the sound of voices below her window. She got up and looked out. A low black and silver car was drawn up outside the gate, and standing beside it was Vicki and a young man – she recognized him as the Jon of the photograph. He wore a duffle coat, and a scarf wound casually round his neck. The two of them were talking quite loudly, so that she couldn't help hearing.

'You scared us stiff,' exclaimed Jon, 'disappearing like that!'

'But what I can't understand is how you knew I had "disappeared" as you call it,' said Vicki.

'Because,' said Jon, 'when I got home, I suddenly remembered that you were counting on me to drive you home and that you might be short of cash—'

'It's a pity you didn't think of that before you left,' Vicki told him. 'It would have saved me an awful lot of bother. But anyway, carry on. What then?'

'I stayed the night with Gran, and all next day I walked on the moors, thinking things out. Then, in the evening, I rang you up to wish you luck before the performance, but evidently you'd already gone. Anyway, there was no answer.'

'We were all at the ballet,' said Vicki. 'Even the Hewetts – both of them.'

'I was about desperate by this time, I can tell you,' continued Jon. 'I decided to have a last shot at getting in touch with you. So I called again on Saturday and got hold of Mrs Hewett. She was just off to Carlisle, she said, and you'd gone out for a walk, but she thought you'd planned to leave Keswick on the Tuesday. I told her to tell you I'd be over for you on the Monday, and she said she'd give you the message. So, on Sunday, I drove over to Newcastle to see some friends, and then I set off for Keswick.'

'I wonder which road you came?' said Vicki half to herself.

'Alston and over Hartside,' answered Jon. 'Why do you want to know?'

'Oh, nothing – I just wondered, that's all.'

'I got to Keswick in the afternoon,' went on Jon, 'and I drove straight to Brocklethwaite. I must say I got the shock of my sweet young life to find it bolted and barred against me! Had to break into my own house! And then, when I had climbed through the larder window, there was no one there at all. No housekeeper, no gardener, no Vicki! It was obvious you weren't just out for a walk, because the Aga was out, and the milk was on the door-step. You'd all disappeared into thin air! It made me feel strange, I can tell you, as if I was living in a fairy story, where the castle and all concerned disappear in a puff of smoke, or a wave of the magician's wand. To make matters even worse (you'll never believe it, I know), someone had been sleeping in my bed – I'll swear it! . . . What's the matter, Vicki? There's nothing to laugh about.'

'Oh, yes, there is,' giggled Vicki. 'When you hear the whole story, you'll see the joke, Jon. It sounds frightfully like *The Three Bears*, doesn't it . . . "Who's been sleeping in *my* bed?" But go on – I'm enjoying every minute of this! What did you do next?'

'Went to bed,' said Jon laconically. 'I made up my mind that you had decided to go home a day early, and that the Hewetts had taken the opportunity of having a little holiday (though, I must say it wasn't like them), and that they'd probably be back in the morning. But next morning came, and there wasn't a sign of them. I cooked my breakfast on the electric stove in solitary splendour. I did a spot of painting during the morning, expecting any minute that you or, more likely, the Hewetts, would turn up. While I was having my lonely lunch I turned on the radio for some news. Then I heard the announcer asking for information about a missing girl. My heart nearly stopped beating – I thought for a moment it was *you*, Vicki, but of course, after he gave the particulars, I realized it couldn't be. All the same, I still felt uneasy, especially when the announcer said that foul play couldn't be ruled out. I kept thinking about my bed, and the person who had slept in it. I can tell you it wasn't a nice feeling! And then there was the disappearance of the Hewetts. At length I couldn't stand it any longer. I hared down to the police station, and told them that *you* were missing, and that our housekeeper and her husband had vanished too. A fat lot of sympathy I got in that quarter! They told me that the Hewetts were in Carlisle Infirmary with concussion after a car accident, and that *that* was why there was no one in the house. I explained to them about my bed, but they just laughed. Suggested I'd slept in it myself before I dashed away, and that Mrs Hewett had forgotten to make it. I ask you! Can you imagine old Hewett going off on a jaunt to Carlisle, leaving any of the beds unmade? Very likely, I *don't* think!'

'And what about *me*? What did they say about me?' demanded Vicki.

'Oh, you? They dismissed you with a flip of the handcuffs, as you might say! Thought you'd turn up in due course, and they happened to be right.'

'Only partly right,' declared Vicki. 'But never mind – I'll explain later on. After that I suppose you came back home.'

'Yes. There was the dickens of a mist, so I thought I'd go via Carlisle and along the Military. Rather straighter road than over Hartside, also more chance of white lines. I thought that the mist might thin out a bit when I left the Lake District behind, but it didn't. If anything, it got thicker. Frankly it was a nightmare!'

'You've said it!' exclaimed Vicki. 'Nightmare is the word!'

Jon stared at her.

'But how on earth did *you* know?'

'Never mind – carry on with the story. You were just crashing along the Military Road—'

'*Crawling* along it would be more accurate,' said Jon. 'Well, when I got to the jolly old Twice Brewed the visibility was down to about nil, so I stopped there and had a meal, hoping conditions would improve. But they didn't, so I just had to go on—'

'Then it *was* you we saw leaving the Twice Brewed!' exclaimed Vicki. 'I told Nona it was a sportscar just like yours, but I never really thought it *was* yours, Jon!'

'Vicki,' said Jon. 'What *are* you hiding? You've been up to some mischief! Who is "we", and who is "Nona"? How did you happen to be at, or near, the Twice Brewed in that mist at night? And finally what are you doing here?'

'What a lot of questions!' laughed Vicki. 'I'll answer them all some day. And I suppose that's the end of your story? You just came back here, rang up my parents, and got them in the dickens of a flap for nothing. Even poor old Trixie!'

'It's all very well—' began Jon, but Vicki cut him short.

'I know! You were in a dreadful "spot",' she admitted. 'I suppose I shall have to forgive you – on one condition.'

'What's that?'

'That you go away now, like a good boy, and leave me in peace,' said Vicki. 'I'm very busy just at the moment. And if you *could* ring up the police and tell them I've turned up, that I'm quite OK and that they can write me off their Missing Girl files, I'd be so grateful! It's not a nice feeling, being trailed by the police!'

'I'll do that,' promised Jon.

Chapter 7

Dress Rehearsal

There's a theory in the theatrical world that a bad dress rehearsal ensures a good performance. In that case, the audience at the Mary Martin Summer Show were going to have a treat next day, for everything that could go wrong at the dress rehearsal had gone wrong! The tiny children were excited and naughty, and kept pinching and pushing each other, until more than one of them was led off the stage in tears to spend the rest of the rehearsal sitting on its mother's knee. Cecil Davenport (who had misbehaved on a former occasion as the Wolf) was even worse as a Huntsman in *Robin Hood*. This didn't come until the second half of the programme, but that didn't stop Cecil from parading with his bow and arrow, and 'shooting' several timid, bare-legged little girls, who stood in the wings shivering in their short costumes and nearly frightening them to death.

The first three rows of stalls were filled with mums and relatives of the performers, not to mention quite a few dads. Over their knees were carefully laid the fluffy white shawls or cross-overs in which to envelop little June, or Mavis, or Pat, the moment she came off-stage after her 'number'. One couldn't be too careful, you see, for little June was (in her proud parents' eyes at any rate) a budding Pavlova, or a potential Fonteyn, and must have great care taken of her. As a matter of fact, Mary (sitting in the Staff box beside Veronica and Sebastian Scott) was thinking much the same thing. Not even *she* knew which child was going to come to the top, though she had a shrewd idea which *wouldn't*. It wouldn't be June, she thought, or Mavis, or Pat, but on the other hand, there *were* children – Her thoughts flew distressingly to the little orphan, Nona Browning. Now *that* child might have gone forward and become a dancer of the first rank; she had the right physical attributes (all except for that unfortunate disfigurement to her face); she had the strong, supple feet and expressive hands; above all, she had the right approach to her work – humble, yet dedicated – the only proper approach to a great art like ballet . . . Oh, well, it was no use dwelling on what might have been. The facts were that Nona had left the Mary Martin school for ever. The child would forget her dancing, and learn to be a good domestic servant or typist, or whatever it was she was doing. Mary sighed.

'Why the sigh, Mary, dear?' asked Sebastian curiously.

'I was just thinking of something rather sad,' confessed Mary.

'I'd like to bet it had something to do with these brats of yours?' said Sebastian.

'Well, yes, it had,' admitted Mary. 'How well you know me!' She turned to Veronica. 'Now comes the bit of real ballet for the Advanced students – Act Two of *Giselle* – the thing you wanted to see.' Mary considered that Veronica (like so many other mothers) was being fussy. Vicki, in her opinion, was quite capable of interpreting the rôle of Giselle in her own way, and wouldn't thank her mother for interference, but she was far too polite and diplomatic to say so.

They waited for the scenery to be changed. One of the students brought Miss Martin and her guests cups of tea. Down in the stalls, the young children had been rounded up and packed off home, accompanied by their exhausted mothers, who, on this afternoon of the dress rehearsal, were asking each other if it was 'worth it'. Tomorrow, after a wonderful performance, they would be saying, 'I wouldn't have missed it for the world! Little Jennifer was *too* sweet in that tiny ballet dress, and your Gillian did well, too, Mrs Lightfoot. I always said that Gillian would make a dancer – always provided she doesn't grow too big. She's head and shoulders over our Jennifer, of course, but then our Jennifer has such small bones; she's like a little bird is our Jennifer. Oh, yes, there *is* a couple of years between them, I know, but I don't think your Gillian was ever quite as small as our Jennifer – not even two years ago. But of course you never know, dear. Your Gillian may stop growing – though I must say it doesn't look like it at present!'

Oh, the jealousy between the mums, the aunts and the cousins! (The dads were never so bad, for some reason, thought Mary). The children themselves were more reasonable. For one thing they were too busy, and too tired to be jealous of each other. Besides, most of them were knowledgable enough to estimate their own, and their fellow students' talents more or less correctly . . . 'Oh, Mum! You mustn't say that about Sheila! Why, she's oceans better than any of us. She got honours in the Intermediate, and that takes some getting, I can tell you! Oh, I know I got honours in Grade Five, but that's different altogether. The Intermediate is a real professional exam, not like the Grades. Everyone thinks Sheila will be accepted for the Royal Ballet School next year. Oh, I know her *mother*'s awful, but you can't blame Sheila for that, and it's got nothing to do with her dancing. Surely you can see that, Mum! . . . '

But jealous mums never see anything. The theatre seethed with emotions and pent-up feelings . . . 'Our Jennifer ought to be . . . our Gillian never was . . . not fair the way they push that little June Smurthwaite . . . that awful child, Hilda Mason, has had her hair permed. The very idea – she can't be more than ten! . . . they say the Rutherford kid has been accepted for the Royal Ballet School. What? Not Hazel Rutherford? Well, I *am* surprised! Personally I don't think she can touch our Marion . . . '

The world of the theatre, the backstage atmosphere with its jealousies and frustrations, had touched even the dress rehearsal of the Mary Martin Summer Show!

Oblivious of these cross-currents, as always, Veronica Weston sat beside her husband and waited patiently for her daughter to appear. The curtain rises on a stage made misty by gauze drop-curtains. There is a back-cloth of mountains and a mediaeval castle, with Giselle's grave, topped with a large cross at the centre-right. All this was painted by Mary's nephew, who was a student at the art school.

And now a veiled figure, Myrtha, Queen of the Wilis, appears and moves swiftly behind the gauze curtains. With two branches held in her outstretched hands, she consecrates the grove to the rites about to take place there. She summons the other Wilis. They enter, veiled, their arms folded on their breasts. They dance off, to return without their veils. They dance again.

Myrtha advances to the cross and, holding out a branch of myrtle, she summons Giselle from her grave. Giselle appears from behind the flower-strewn mound where the cross is erected. She is veiled also, her eyes are closed, and her arms crossed on her breast. She dances before the Queen, who disappears into the woods. Giselle expresses her joy at returning to the world . . .

'Why,' exclaimed Veronica, 'Poor Myrtha must be suffering badly from stage-fright – she's forgotten to pluck off Giselle's veil! Fortunately it doesn't matter, as it's only the dress rehearsal . . . I must say Vicki is dancing beautifully – so lyrically! I had no idea she put such feeling into her work.'

163

'Nor had I, now you come to mention it,' commented Sebastian.

Mary said nothing. She was puzzled. First of all, there was Myrtha. Hilda Steinberg, who was dancing the rôle, was a girl of iron nerves, and most unlikely to suffer from stage-fright. Then there was Giselle herself – there was something about her dancing Mary couldn't understand. Vicki's dancing was brilliant, technically perfect, but it had always lacked sympathy. It was as if she was dancing with her head, and not with her heart. But today – why, she was quite beautiful! There was something else that puzzled Mary – the dancer was making mistakes. Not anything that really mattered, of course, but one would almost think she didn't know the rôle. Vicki never made mistakes. It was all very strange. A pucker of bewilderment appeared between Mary's eyebrows.

'Well,' observed Veronica, 'I really don't know what Vicki wanted me to advise her about. I might say she could do with a little more rehearsing, perhaps – she's not quite sure of the entrances and exits, is she? But apart from that, she dances beautifully – quite beautifully.' She gave a little sigh of pleasure. 'I see my dream coming true before my eyes – the dream that I might see my daughter take my place when I am too old to dance any longer. I must confess,' she added to Mary, 'I have sometimes had my doubts.'

'So have I,' confessed Sebastian. 'Matter of fact, I still have. Unless I am much mistaken, that girl who is dancing Giselle so very beautifully and sensitively, is *not* Vicki at all!'

'You are right as usual, Papa,' said a voice from the back of the box. 'It is *not* Vicki.'

The words caused a sensation, as well they might. Veronica was shattered. Not so Mary – she'd known, really, all the time.

'Then who on earth is it?' demanded Veronica.

'Don't *you* know?' said Vicki, turning to Mary. 'Can't *you* guess why the Queen of the Wilis couldn't pluck off Giselle's veil? (and gosh, what a job I had to persuade her to "forget"!) I should have thought it was obvious.'

'Of course I can guess,' Mary said with fast-beating heart. (It looked as if one of *her* dreams was going to come true this time.) 'It's little Nona Browning!'

This announcement meant nothing at all to Veronica and Sebastian, of course, since they had never heard of Nona, and therefore knew nothing about her disfigurement. They watched the dancer in silence for some minutes; then Sebastian said, 'Well, I suppose Vicki, your idea was that we should see this dancer, though why you should make such a mystery out of it, and why she should have to dance in your place, and what the veil has to do with it, I can't begin to imagine.'

'You'll see in a minute,' said Vicki. 'Look it's finished now—' Giselle had disappeared behind the grassy mound with one last wave of her white arm. 'Just stay here for a moment, all of you. I want you – and Mama especially – to meet Giselle.'

Chapter 8

Vicki's Plan

They sat waiting, and then a white-clad figure, still veiled, appeared at the back of the box. She was breathing hard, partly because she had just come off stage, and partly because she was very frightened. Never had she thought to stand face to face with two such famous people as Veronica Weston and Sebastian Scott. Besides, she knew that her whole life depended upon this interview.

'Mama and Papa,' said Vicki, 'I want you to meet Nona Browning!' She drew Nona forward, and at the same time lifted her veil. '*Now* do you understand why I had to do what I did? You had to see her dance before you saw her face . . . Mummy,' (she dropped into her childhood's form of addressing her mother) 'will you do something for me? Will you adopt Nona, and let her do all the things you have dreamed up for me? *Please* Mummy!'

'Vicki! What do you mean?' cried Veronica.

'I think I know,' put in Sebastian quietly. 'Fathers sometimes understand their daughters better than mothers do. Mothers are sometimes too close to see properly. Vicki is trying to tell us, my darling, that she doesn't want to dance. Isn't that so, Vicki? I've suspected it for some time now. I even think I know what it is you really want to do.'

'Clever, clever Papa!' cried Vicki, making a little bow. 'But let's not talk of *me* now. I can manage my own affairs. But with Nona it's different. She's so shy and silent (because you see she finds it so difficult to talk), and so gentle. Please, Mama, I want you to help Nona, and then

I won't feel so bad about not following you as a dancer. You remember one night you and Papa were talking to the Rounthwaites – Sylvia and Peter – about Sir James Hartly, the plastic surgeon, and the miracles he performs. You even mentioned somebody with a hare-lip. Oh, I know he's terribly expensive, but you and Papa have loads of money—'

'Have we?' repeated Sebastian mildly. 'I didn't think anyone had loads of money nowadays!'

'Well, you'd do it at once if it were *me* that had the hare-lip,' said Vicki. 'You know you would! So please do it for Nona – for my sake. She could live at dear Lady Bailey's. (Lady Bailey would *adore* her; you remember how she cosseted Ella Rosetti when she was ill?) and she could go to classes with Madame Viret and my darling Maestro – they've got imagination, and they'd see at once what she's going to be. I think we shouldn't spring her upon the Royal Ballet School until she's quite cured, and that will take two years at least.'

'I see you've got it all worked out!' said Sebastian. He looked at his only daughter with admiration. 'I expect it will work out exactly as you say! But we shall have to have some talk with Miss Martin about all this, and *you*,' he turned to Nona, 'I suppose you are all in favour?'

Nona murmured something that none of them, except Vicki, understood, but her shining eyes told them just what she thought about it.

'Come here, child, and don't be afraid,' said Veronica softly. 'You look scared to death! Your dancing pleased me immensely. You were quite beautiful!'

'Thank you, miss – madam—' stammered Nona. She blushed nervously.

'And make no mistake about it,' went on Veronica, 'we shall have that poor lip cured. You will work hard while it is being done?'

'Oh, I will indeed, madam,' said Nona.

'My name is Veronica Weston,' said the dancer gently. 'Or perhaps better still Mrs Scott. I've been thinking lately that perhaps I've been too much Veronica Weston, and not enough Mrs Scott! Someone told me that my only daughter was often lonely . . .'

'Oh, Mummy – I don't know who told you that,' said Vicki. 'Was it Jon?'

'It doesn't matter who it was,' answered Veronica. 'The important thing is whether or not it is true.'

'I do sometimes want you, Mummy,' admitted Vicki.

'My poor darling!' cried her mother. 'I'm afraid both your father and I are so self-centred . . .'

'Oh, Mama – *not* self-centred!' exclaimed Vicki, horrified. 'Let's say single-minded.'

'Which is a more polite way of saying the same thing!' laughed Sebastian. 'Well, your mother and I have decided to see a lot more of you, Vicki, in the future. I imagine that at the Slade you will have more time on your hands than at the Royal Ballet School – more leisure to devote to *us*; and we, in our turn, will see to it that we have more time for *you*. Your mother has decided to do no more tours abroad for one thing.'

'Oh, Papa' cried Vicki – 'you've guessed what it is I want to be. An artist! I think I've wanted it all my life! You really mean I can study at the Slade; and then Paris, and perhaps Italy? Oh, Papa and Mama – I'm so very happy!'

Veronica and Sebastian looked at each other. Neither of them had ever seen Vicki like this before – so natural, and vivacious.

'Oh, what a wonderful dancer she would have made!' thought Veronica sadly. 'But then, she never looked like this when she was dancing.' It seems, she thought, that whatever you do, your heart must be in it – whether you are a secretary, a bus-conductor, or selling something in a shop. And especially is this true in some of the more exacting professions – nursing, for instance, music and ballet. These demand a special measure of whole-heartedness, so it was, perhaps, a good thing that Vicki had found out in time where her heart lay.

Mary, sitting at the back of the box, heard them talking – discussing how soon Nona could go to London; how to square the orphanage authorities, and how to explain to the police.

'How I shall enjoy telling that old so-and-so, General Whatever-his-name-is just where to get off!' said Sebastian wickedly. 'Never shall I have enjoyed myself more!'

'Well,' put in Mary Martin, 'the theatre is empty now. The dress rehearsal is over, so I suggest we all go home.'

'So do I,' said Vicki. 'For one thing, I'm longing for a hot bath! Nona will come home with us, won't you, Nona? . . . By the way, I tried on the Giselle costume you had made for me, Miss Martin, and it's perfect. I thought I'd better be sure because of course I shall be dancing tomorrow in the show – though I shan't do it half as well as Nona! It's been such an important dress rehearsal that I'd almost forgotten we hadn't yet had the actual performance!'

Epilogue

Another year has passed, and we are in Lady Bailey's house in Carsbroke Place, London. Lady Bailey has had a big studio made on the top floor, and here, standing in front of a mirror is a young girl. Nothing very strange about that, you may say; young girls often stand in front of mirrors! Yes, but there is something different about this mirror – there is a veil of chiffon over it, so that the girl cannot see her face in it. She stands there, obviously trying to make up her mind to tear down the veil. She puts out her hand, then draws it back again.

At last she summons up all her courage, takes a deep breath, and pulls down the piece of chiffon. Her face looks back at her, dark-eyed, framed with soft, silken, brown hair. Her mouth is curved sweetly and sensitively. She looks closer into the mirror, and sees a tiny scar on her upper lip – all that is left of her disfigurement! A touch of powder, and it will not be seen at all.

'Thank you, God,' she says, clasping her hands together. 'I asked you to help me once, remember? I thought you had quite forgotten, but you hadn't!' The low tones of her voice are still a little indistinct but dancers, like flowers, are not expected to speak, so this does not matter and at least there is no difficulty in making out what she is saying. 'And I hope, dear God,' went on Nona, 'that you will help Vicki to realize *her* dream of being a painter, because if it hadn't been for Vicki, I should never have been cured . . . And that reminds me,' she added, 'I must ring Vicki up – it's her birthday – her eighteenth – and she's spending it in Northumberland.'

While Nona was standing in front of her mirror, admiring

the work of the plastic surgeon, Vicki and Jon were leaning over the bottom half of the stable door, where Vicki's pony Maestro, was munching hay.

'You remember,' said Jon, 'years ago, when we were riding on the moors, I asked you to marry me. I said that when you were eighteen, I should want my answer. Well, you're eighteen today, Vicki, so what is it to be?'

'Oh, Jon!' laughed Vicki. 'Really, you are a most tenacious boy! How can I give you an answer when I don't know myself? But at all events – you may kiss me.' She stood with her eyes tightly shut, waiting, but nothing happened.

'When I want to kiss you, I shall do so,' said Jon stiffly. 'I won't wait for you to ask me. So, my dear, until you have found the answer to my question, I shall go on waiting. Some day – I know it, Vicki, the answer will be "yes".'

'I have an idea it will, too!' answered Vicki.

Lorna Hill
A Dream of Sadler's Wells £2.99

When tragedy strikes, will her dreams be buried for ever?

With the death of her father, fourteen-year-old Veronica Weston is suddenly uprooted from her life in London and the ballet classes she loves so much. The prospect of a new life in the north of England seems to shatter her dream of becoming a great dancer.

But on the train to Northumberland she makes a friend who has a secret wish of his own. In the adventures that follow, Veronica realizes that it will take all her determination to succeed in the rigorous world of ballet – and that begins with running away from home . . .

Principal Role £2.99

Life can be full of danger – even for a princess

After five years in exile Crown Princess Fazia joins the famous Royal Ballet School. Her dream is not to be a ballerina, but to be free like other girls – able to go where and how she pleases.

One day, during an eventful Christmas in the north of England, Fazia escapes the royal bodyguard and sets off alone. But life as an ordinary girl is not as easy as Fazia had thought it would be – and who will take her place in the role for which she was destined?

Sadler's Wells
Lorna Hill
Swan Feather £2.99

Dancers are notoriously superstitious, and Sylvia was no exception
to the rule. She believed implicitly in the magical properties of her
swan feather. But she was to find that, although it may be a
comforting thing to have a mascot when one is young and unsure of
oneself, it is talent and sheer hard work that gets one to the top of
one's profession – not a mere swan's feather!

This is the story of Sylvia Swan, and also of Vicki (young daughter
of Veronica and Sebastian Scott) both of whom are studying at the
Royal Ballet School. In her adventures Sylvia stays at Vicki's home,
Bracken Hall in Northumberland, and meets many of Vicki's friends –
among them Mariella Campbell and Jane Charlton. Also Sir Nigel
Monkhouse, young squire of Bychester, and his redoubtable mother,
who are definitely *not* numbered among Vicki's friends!

All Pan books are available at your local bookshop or newsagent, or can be ordered direct from the publisher. Indicate the number of copies required and fill in the form below.

Send to: **CS Department, Pan Books Ltd., P.O. Box 40, Basingstoke, Hants.   RG21 2YT.**

or phone: 0256 469551 (Ansaphone), quoting title, author and Credit Card number.

Please enclose a remittance* to the value of the cover price plus: 60p for the first book plus 30p per copy for each additional book ordered to a maximum charge of £2.40 to cover postage and packing.

*Payment may be made in sterling by UK personal cheque, postal order, sterling draft or international money order, made payable to Pan Books Ltd.

Alternatively by Barclaycard/Access:

Card No.

Signature:

Applicable only in the UK and Republic of Ireland.

While every effort is made to keep prices low, it is sometimes necessary to increase prices at short notice. Pan Books reserve the right to show on covers and charge new retail prices which may differ from those advertised in the text or elsewhere.

NAME AND ADDRESS IN BLOCK LETTERS PLEASE:

....

Name ——————————————————————

Address ——————————————————————

——————————————————————

——————————————————————

——————————————————————

3/87